NAIMA SIMONE

RUTHLESS PRIDE

HARLEQUIN
DESIRE

To Gary. 143.

Special thanks and acknowledgment are given
to Naima Simone for her contribution to the
Dynasties: Seven Sins miniseries.

Recycling programs
for this product may
not exist in your area.

ISBN-13: 978-1-335-20909-2

Ruthless Pride

Copyright © 2020 by Harlequin Books S.A.

This edition published by arrangement with Harlequin Books S.A.

For questions and comments about the quality of this book,
please contact us at CustomerService@Harlequin.com.

Harlequin Enterprises ULC
22 Adelaide St. West, 40th Floor
Toronto, Ontario M5H 4E3, Canada
www.Harlequin.com

Printed in U.S.A.

USA TODAY bestselling author **Naima Simone**'s love of romance was first stirred by Harlequin books pilfered from her grandmother. Now she spends her days writing sizzling romances with a touch of humor and snark.

She is wife to her own real-life superhero and mother to two awesome kids. They live in perfect, domestically challenged bliss in the southern United States.

Books by Naima Simone

Harlequin Desire

Blackout Billionaires

The Billionaire's Bargain
Black Tie Billionaire
Blame It on the Billionaire

Dynasties: Seven Sins

Ruthless Pride

Visit her Author Profile page at Harlequin.com, or naimasimone.com, for more titles.

You can also find Naima Simone on Facebook, along with other Harlequin Desire authors, at Facebook.com/harlequindesireauthors!

Dear Reader,

I'm a PK—a pastor's kid. So I know a little something about sins. LOL! When I found out my very first continuity would be based on the seven sins? Kismet, right? We were totally made for each other!

In *Ruthless Pride*, Joshua Lowell is the oldest son of the infamous Vernon Lowell. When Vernon disappeared with millions of his clients' money, he left his family—specifically, Joshua—to pick up the pieces. For fifteen years, Joshua has tried to repair the damage his father caused. Pride has kept him in the town of Falling Brook when he could've left like his brothers. And pride has him going head-to-head with the journalist of the local newspaper. She wants to resurrect the old history that he wants everyone to forget. He should resent stubborn, ambitious and beautiful Sophie Armstrong. And he does. But only if he could stop wanting her, too...

Oh, yes. They're adversaries, but these two can't stay away from each other. I hope you enjoy all the steam and drama they generate! And I hope you love the Seven Sins series!

Happy reading!

Naima Simone

Seven Sins

One man's betrayal can destroy generations.

*Ten years ago, a hedge-fund hotshot vanished
with billions, leaving the high-powered families
of Falling Brook changed forever.*

*Now seven heirs, shaped by his betrayal,
must reckon with the sins of the past.*

Passion may be their only path to redemption.

Experience all Seven Sins!

* * *

Ruthless Pride by Naima Simone

This CEO's pride led him to give up his dreams
for his family. Now he's drawn to the woman
who threatens everything...

Forbidden Lust by Karen Booth

He's always resisted his lust for his best friend's sister—
until they're stranded together in paradise...

Insatiable Hunger by Yahrah St. John

His unbridled appetite for his closest friend is unleashed
when he believes she's fallen for the wrong man...

Hidden Ambition by Jules Bennett

Ambition has taken him far, but revenge could
cost him his one chance at love...

Reckless Envy by Joss Wood

When this shark in the boardroom meets the one
woman he can't have, envy takes over...

Untamed Passion by Cat Schield

Will this black sheep's self-destructive wrath flame
out when he's expecting an heir of his own?

Slow Burn by Janice Maynard

If he's really the idle playboy his family claims,
will his inaction threaten a reunion with
the woman who got away?

"I would've noticed you..."

A liquid slide of lust prowled through Joshua like a hungry—so goddamn hungry—beast. The air simmered around them.

"Do you want me to prove that I'm not some kind of stalker?" Sophie tilted her head to the side. "I'm dedicated to my job, but I refuse to cross the line into creepy...or criminal."

He ground his teeth against the apology that shoved at his throat. "I'm sorry. I shouldn't have jumped to conclusions." And then he added, "That predilection seems to be in the air."

A tiny muscle ticked along her delicate but stubborn jaw. "And what is that supposed to mean?"

Moments earlier, Joshua had wondered if fury or desire had heated Sophie's gaze.

God help him, because masochistic fool that he'd suddenly become, he craved them both.

He wanted her rage, her passion...wanted both to beat at him, heat his skin, touch him.

To make him feel.

* * *

Ruthless Pride by Naima Simone is part of the Dynasties: Seven Sins series.

One

"*If your success was earned through hard work and honesty never apologize for it.*"

Joshua Lowell silently repeated the Frank Sonnenberg quote that had been a favorite of his father's. He pinched the bridge of his nose, a low, dark growl rumbling in the back of his throat. Too bad Vernon Lowell hadn't believed in the "practice what you preach" school of thought. According to that quote, his father had a ton of apologizing to do. Wherever he was—hell or a bungalow in some country without extradition policies.

Dropping his head, he refocused his attention to the spreadsheets displaying the previous month's profit-and-loss numbers for Black Crescent Hedge Fund's investment in stock of a telecommunication company. Compared with this time last year, the investment was doing very well. Their clients would earn more than a modest return, and Black Crescent would receive a substantial management and performance fee...

Unlike his father, Joshua had stuck to the more traditional investments such as stocks, bonds, commodities and real estate. Vernon had been a daredevil in business, which initially had made him one of the richest men in the tristate area of New York, New Jersey and Connecticut. That fearless and adventurous spirit had also increased the millions his very select clients had invested with him into high-yielding portfolios, and grew his boutique business into one of most successful in the area.

It'd also cost those select clients millions. It'd devastated them.

So no, while some might call Joshua's business decisions rigid and even too conservative, he refused to do anything different. Too many people's livelihoods and futures depended on him making those safe choices. He refused to be another Lowell who betrayed their trust. Who destroyed them.

He'd been the last man standing when Vernon Lowell disappeared—for both the company and his family. Because he'd left with not only his clients' money, but the majority of his family's, as well. So even though the last man sometimes wanted to yell and rage at the unfairness of it all, at the grief and shame that often pounded within him like a second heartbeat—at the death of his own dreams—one thing the last man *couldn't* do was slip up or falter.

He couldn't afford to. Literally.

"Josh, did you hear what I said? Of course you didn't." Haley Shaw, his executive assistant, snorted, answering her own question before he could respond. "Or you're just ignoring me, which you should know by now doesn't work. Whatever you're doing now can be put aside for just a few moments. This is important," she insisted, an edge invading her tone.

"Haley. Not now," he said without glancing up from his spreadsheet.

"Well, I'm sorry to interrupt," a brisk, husky but very feminine voice that carried zero hint of apology interjected, "but I'm afraid it's going to have to be now."

Two small hands with slender, unadorned fingers flattened on either side of his computer monitor. Surprised, all he could do for several long seconds was stare at those delicate hands. At the short, unpolished nails, the thin map of light blue veins under sun-kissed skin. Why did he have the odd but strong urge to place his mouth right on the joint where hand met wrist—and sip?

Hell. They were fucking hands.

The mental but mocking admonishment didn't stop him from traveling up the lengths of her arms clad in white sleeves to slim shoulders partially hidden by light brown and gold-streaked hair, past a graceful neck and slightly pointed but stubborn chin with its slight indent to a face that—*goddamn.*

Deliberately, he eased back in his office chair, careful to control all the muscles in his face. He forced himself to maintain the cold, aloof expression that he'd adopted and mastered fifteen years ago as a defense. But inside…inside, lust slammed into him like a hurricane intent on leveling every structure in its path. And right now he was the only thing remaining, and *Christ*, he was shaking right down to his foundation.

Thickly lashed silver eyes that gleamed with barely suppressed anger. Striking cheekbones that lent a bold strength to otherwise ethereal features. A gently sloped nose and a mouth that had him gripping the arms of his chair like they were the last lifeboat that kept him from drowning. Thing was, he wanted to leap from the safety of the raft and dive into that wide, full-lipped mouth. Teach it what it was created for. Show it how it could give both of them the filthiest of pleasures…

His heartbeat echoed its thundering rhythm in his cock, pounding out a need that ricocheted through him.

Unsettled by his visceral reaction to this stranger—a stranger who had barged into his corporate office uninvited—he narrowed his eyes on her, allowing the corners of his mouth to curl in a derisive snarl.

Haley heaved a sigh. "Joshua, let me introduce you to Sophie Armstrong," she said, a thick coat of resignation painting her words.

"I don't know a Sophie Armstrong," he stated coldly to his assistant, although he didn't remove his gaze from the woman in front of him. Maybe some instinctual part of him recognized that she was the biggest threat in the room—a threat to his schedule, his carefully laid-out day…his control.

"The name would be familiar if you bothered to answer any one of my phone calls or emails." She snorted, cocking a dark eyebrow. "I've been trying to contact you, Mr. Lowell, and you've ducked and dodged every attempt."

He frowned. Yes, he'd been busier than usual lately, but he would've remembered if she'd reached out to him. "I've never ducked or dodged anyone." Not even when he'd desperately longed to. "Especially someone who doesn't have enough manners or sense to not force herself into a place of business where she wasn't invited or wanted without an appointment. Now that you're here, you have exactly thirty seconds—twenty-nine more seconds than I would give anyone else—to explain what the hell you're talking about."

Others would've—had—recoiled and backed down from the hard, ice-cold fury in his voice. But Sophie Armstrong didn't even flinch. Instead, she met his glare with one of her own. A quicksilver flash of surprise flickered within him. He wasn't arrogant, but he also acknowledged his appeal to the opposite sex. Understanding his money proved just as much of a lure as the appearance he'd inherited from his handsome father, he never lacked for female attention. Or sex.

But to this woman, he might as well be Quasimodo

taking a break from his Notre Dame tower to hang out in the Black Crescent offices. Sophie Armstrong didn't bother to employ any advantage her beauty might press—not that it would. But she didn't know that.

No, unless antagonism passed for charm these days, she was confrontational and contemptuous.

And goddamn, if it wasn't hot.

She reached into the bag over her shoulder, withdrew a stack of papers and slapped the pile on his desk. "That's what I'm talking about. All the emails I've sent you. And I can pull out my phone and scroll through and play every voice mail—there are fifteen of them. All asking you to reply in a timely manner. Apparently, your idea of timely and mine don't coincide because I meant at least a couple of days and yours apparently runs along the line of seasons in Narnia."

The snort slipped from him before he could contain it. He shouldn't be amused. And he certainly shouldn't let her see it.

"You have five seconds left," he informed her, leaning forward and with a will that had been forged in the fires of desperation, humiliation and pride over a decade ago, he shifted his attention back to his screen. "I suggest you make the most of it."

A soft, feminine growl filled the air, and the reverberation of it rolled in his gut, clenching the muscles there so hard he nearly grunted in pain. With the wrenching came the dark but HD-clear image of her, head thrown back, all that hair sprawled across black sheets, beads of sweat dotting the slender column of her throat. And that same, rumbling growl vibrating from her. Only it sounded hungrier, needier...

Christ, he needed her out of his office.

"I'm assuming that king-of-the-manor-got-no-time-for-peasants thing intimidates other people, but I hate to break it to you. It does nothing for me." She crossed her arms over her chest, and if Jesus had come down at that moment and warned him against giving in to his baser needs, Joshua still wouldn't have been able to stop his gaze from dipping to the slightly less-than-a-handful but firm breasts that pushed against the plain white dress shirt. Guilt streaked through him, slick and dirty. He wasn't his father; he didn't ogle women or treat them like eye candy, there for his pleasure. Even women who made his dick hard but he didn't particularly like. "I'm telling you now—like I did in my last voice message and two emails—I'll be writing my story with or without you. But it would be a better one *with* you."

Story. What *story*?

A sense of foreboding wormed its way into his chest, hollowing it out. Making room for the churning unease.

"I repeat," he stated, the flat tone revealing none of the steadily encroaching panic that crept into his vision, that squeezed his rib cage like a steadily tightening vise. "What are you talking about?"

"The anniversary piece on the Black Crescent fiasco that I'm writing for the *Falling Brook Chronicle*. And unlike all of the articles written about that time period, I would like to include an interview with the company's current CEO."

Anger crystallized within him, hard and diamond bright. And sharp enough to cut glass. The "get out" burned on his tongue, singeing him. But he extinguished the words before they could escape him, refusing to betray any emotion to this woman who sought to rip open the seams of the past, to expose old but unhealed wounds for public consumption. To relive the nightmare of his father emptying the family bank accounts as well as embezzling millions from his clients and disappearing, abandoning him, his mother and brothers to the wolves. The abrasive rub of judging eyes and not-so-hushed whispers. The smothering guilt that ten families were left devastated and destitute because of his father's actions. The agonizing pain from being deceived and abandoned by the man who'd raised him, who'd loved him and who he'd respected.

This woman had no clue about the pressure from the weight of that guilt, that responsibility. How they straddled his shoulders to the point of suffocation at times. How dealing had become second nature to him. There'd been no one to lean on when his father disappeared, when he'd taken on the responsibility of repaying the families so they wouldn't sue for the remaining money his father hadn't disappeared with. When his mother withdrew from the exclusive community of Falling Brook, New Jersey. When his twin brother, Jacob, fled to Europe to backpack his problems away, and his youngest brother, Oliver, dropped out of college and become the poster child for professional playboy, complete with a nasty cocaine habit.

Nothing in his Ivy League education—not even the economic courses he'd taken at his father's insistence—had prepared him for being alone, grieving and terrified with the fate of not just his family but ten others on his still-young shoulders. Of having to make the bitter decision of burying his own dreams so he could repair those of others.

He'd grown up fast. Too fast.

And damn if he needed an article written by an ambitious reporter—no matter if she possessed the face of a fairy queen and the body of a Victoria's Secret Angel—to drag him back to those desolate, black times when he'd breathed fear as much as he did air.

"No."

Joshua gave her credit—she didn't flinch at the flat, blunt answer.

Instead, she tilted her head to the side, that fall of thick caramel-and-sunlight hair sliding over her shoulder, and studied him as if he were a problem to solve. Or an opponent to wrestle and pin into submission.

"I can understand why you would initially be reluctant to speak with me—"

"Oh, you can?" he interrupted, trying but failing to keep the bite from his voice. Silently, he cursed himself for revealing even that much. The last fifteen years had taught him that he couldn't afford to betray the slightest weakness of character lest he be accused of being just like his father. Other people were allowed room for mistakes. He was not offered that courtesy. While others could trip up in private, his missteps were splashed across newspapers and online columns for fodder. Including *her* paper. "So you've had a—how did you so eloquently put it?—fiasco in your life and had every paper in the country report on it? Including the *Falling Brook Chronicle*? Which, if I remember correctly, was one of the harshest and most critical? Well, good," he continued, not granting her the opportunity to answer. "Since you have experienced it, you'll understand why I'm ending this conversation."

"I've read the past articles from the *Chronicle*, and you're right, they did cover it…punitively," she conceded. In the small pause that followed, the "can you blame them?" seemed to echo in the office. "But those reporters aren't me. You don't know me, but I graduated from Northwestern University with a BS and MS in journalism. While there, I worked with the Medill Justice Project that helped free an unjustly convicted man from a life sentence in prison. I've also won the Walter S. and Syrena M. Howell competition, was a recipient of the NJLA's journalism award and was a member of the journalistic team who won the Stuart and Beverly Awbrey Award last year, all well-respected awards. I don't intend to do a hatchet job on you or Black Crescent. As a matter of fact, I would like to write this article from a different angle—the artist submerged. From my research, I discovered you were once a very accomplished artist—"

"We're done," he ground out, rising to his feet, flattening his palms on the desk.

Hell, no. Pain, like crushed glass, scraped his throat and chest raw.

He hadn't been called an artist in fifteen long years. And hadn't picked up a camera or paintbrush in just as long. Once, his trademark had been oversize, mixed-media collages that provided cultural commentary on war and human rights. He'd poured his being into those pieces, falling into endless pockets of time where nothing had mattered but losing himself in photographs, oils and whatever elements captured what swirled inside him—metal, newspapers, books, even bits of clothing. But when his father had vanished, Joshua had put aside childish things. At least that was what Vernon had called Joshua's passion—a childish hobby.

It'd been like performing a lobotomy on his soul. But now, instead of channeling his anger, grief and pain into art, he suppressed it. And when that didn't work, he funneled it into making Black Crescent solvent and powerful again. Or took it out on a punching bag at the gym.

The whole shitfest with the hedge fund had left him with precious little—the death of his art career, the eradication of his relationships with his brothers, a ghost of a mother, an overabundance of shame and a ruined family company. But they'd been *his* choices.

All that had remained in the ashes after the firestorm were the ragged tatters of his pride because he'd had the strength, the character, to make those choices.

And now Sophie Armstrong sought to steal that dignity away from him, too.

No. She couldn't have it.

"Mr. Lowell," she began again with a short shake of her head.

But again, he cut her off. "I have a busy day, and you've had more than the thirty seconds I allotted. We're through talking. You need to go," he ordered, knowing his mother would cringe at the lack of the manners she'd drilled into him since birth. Not that he gave a damn. Not when this woman stood here prying into an area of his life that wasn't open for public consumption.

"Fine, I'll leave," she said, but nothing in the firm, almost combative tone said she'd conceded. She drew her shoulders back, hiking her chin in the air. Though she stood at least a foot shorter than him, she still managed to peer down at him with a glint of battle in her silver eyes. "You can try to erase the past, but certain things don't go away no matter how hard you try to bury them. The truth always finds a way of resurrecting itself."

"Especially if there are reporters always armed with a shovel, ready to dig up anything that will sell papers," he drawled.

The curves of her full mouth flattened, and her eyes went molten. He waited, his body stilling except for the heavy thud of his heart against his rib cage. And the rush of hot anticipation in his veins.

It'd been years since anyone had challenged him. Not since he'd proved he was his father's son in business and, at times, in ruthlessness. But Sophie Armstrong… She must not have received the memo, because she glared at him, slashes of red painting her high cheekbones, as if even now, she longed to go for his throat. Was it perverse that part of him hoped she did? That he wanted that tight, petite, almost fragile body pressed to his larger frame with those delicate but capable-looking hands wrapped around his neck…exerting pressure even as he took her mouth as she attempted to take his breath?

Yeah, that might make him a little sick. And a hell of a lot dirty.

Still… He could picture it easily. Could feel the phantom tightening of her grip now. And he wanted it. Craved it.

But not enough to rip open old, barely scarred-over wounds so she could have a byline.

"Thank you for your time, Mr. Lowell," she finally said, and disappointment at her retreat surged through him.

God, what was wrong with him? He wanted—no, needed—her to drop this "artist submerged" bullshit and get the hell out of his office.

She whirled around on her boring nude heels and stalked across the room to his office door. Without a backward glance, she exited. He half expected her to slam it shut, but somehow the quiet, definite snick of the lock engaging seemed much more ominous.

Like a booming warning shot across his bow.

Two

"*The Black Crescent Scandal: Fifteen Years Later.*"

Joshua gripped the Monday issue of the *Falling Brook Chronicle* so tightly, it should've been torn down the middle. She'd done it. Sophie Armstrong had run with the story, placing his family's sordid and ugly history on the front page as fodder for an always scandal-hungry public.

He lifted his gaze to stare out the windshield of his Mercedes-Benz at the Black Crescent building. He knew every railing, every angle, every stone inch of the modern midcentury building built into a cliff. His father's aim had been for the headquarters of his hedge fund to stand out in the more traditional architecture of Falling Brook. And he'd succeeded. The building was as famous—or infamous—as its owner.

And his infamy had made page one of the local paper. Again.

Studying the imposing structure offered the briefest of respites. Almost against his will, he returned his attention to the newspaper crinkling under his fists. He'd already read the article twice, but he scanned it again. It recounted his father's rise in the financial industry, his seemingly perfect life—marriage to Eve Evans-Janson, the pedigreed society daughter and darling whose connections further installed Vernon as a reigning king of Falling Brook; his three sons, who'd shown great promise with their Ivy League educations and fast-track career goals; the meteoric success of his business. And then his epic fall. Millions of dollars missing from the hedge fund's accounts. The death of Everett Reardon, his father's best friend and CFO of Black Crescent, who'd crashed his car while trying to elude capture. Vernon's disappearance.

The ten clients his father had stolen money from plunged into a nightmare of bankruptcy and destitution. The company's—Joshua's—agreement to pay back the families so they wouldn't file a lawsuit. How some of them still hadn't recovered from Vernon's selfish, unforgivable and criminal actions.

And then Joshua.

The artist turned CEO who had stepped into the vacant shoes of his father to save Black Crescent. Yes, it shared how he'd left his promising art career and turned the company around, saving it from ruin, but it also painted him as Vernon's puppet, coached and raised to take over for him since Joshua's birth.

Which was bullshit. At one time, his path had been different. Had been his.

The article also cited that no one had heard from Vernon in a decade and a half, but despite rumors that he'd been killed in retribution for his crimes, there was also the long-held belief that his father was alive and well. And that his family was secretly in contact with him. That Vernon still pulled the strings, running Black Crescent from some remote location. Which was ridiculous. After his father initially vanished, his mother had hired a team of private detectives to locate him. Not to mention the FBI had searched for him, as well.

Fuck. He gritted his teeth against releasing the roar in his throat, but his head echoed with it. What did he have to do to redeem himself? What more did he have to sacrifice? He'd stayed, facing judgment, scorn and suspicion to rebuild the company, to restore even some of the money lost. He'd stayed, doing his best in the last fifteen years to repay those affected clients at least part of the fortune they'd lost to his father as promised. He'd stayed, enduring his brothers' ridicule and disdain for following in dear old Dad's footsteps. He'd stayed, caring for their mother, who'd become something of a recluse.

He'd stayed when all he'd wanted to do was quit and run away, too.

But he hadn't gallivanted off to Europe or found sweet oblivion in drugs and parties. Pride and loyalty had chained him there. Fatherless. Brotherless. Friendless.

And Sophie Armstrong dared insinuate he hadn't busted his ass all these years? That his father had done all the soul-destroying work.

His sharp bark of laughter rebounded against the interior of the vehicle. Its serrated edges scraped over his skin.

A part of him that could never utter the sacrilegious words aloud secretly hoped Vernon was dead. Just thinking it caused shame, thick and oily, to slide down his throat and smear his chest in a grimy coat. But it was true. He hoped his father no longer lived, because the alternative… God, the alternative—that he'd abandoned his family and emptied their bank accounts without the slightest shred of remorse and never looked back—sat in his gut, curdling it. If Vernon wasn't dead, then that would mean the man he'd loved and had once admired and respected had truly never existed. And with everything else Joshua had endured these past few years, that…that might be his breaking point.

His cell phone rang, and a swift glance at the screen revealed Oliver's number. On the heels of his past staring him in the face this morning, his chest tightened. He and his younger brother's relationship was…complicated. Oliver lived in Falling Brook, but he might as well be across the Hudson River or even farther away.

Once, they'd been close. But that had been before Joshua had stepped in to head Black Crescent in place of their father. He'd lost some respect in Jacob's and

Oliver's eyes that day. And a part of Joshua mourned that loss. Mourned what had been.

Briefly closing his eyes, Joshua slid his thumb across the screen and lifted the phone to his ear.

"Hello."

"I'm assuming you've seen today's paper," his brother said in lieu of a greeting.

"Yes." Joshua stared across the parking lot, no longer seeing the building that had been the blessing and curse on his family. In front of him wavered an image of a perfect family. Of a lie. "I've seen it."

A sound between an angry growl and a heavy sigh reached him. "This shit again. Why can't people just let it die?" Oliver snapped.

"Because it makes for good copy apparently," Joshua drawled. "We'll ride this one out like we always do."

He uttered the assurance, and it tasted like bitter ashes on his tongue. He was tired of weathering storms. And more so of being the stalwart helm in it.

Oliver scoffed. "Right. Because that's what Lowells do." Joshua could easily picture his brother dragging his hand through his hair, a slight sneer twisting his mouth. "Do you know if Mom has seen the article?"

"I don't think so." Joshua shook his head as the stone of another burden settled on his shoulders. "I've sent Haley over to make sure the paper isn't delivered."

Thank God for Haley. She was more than his assistant. She was his taskmaster. Right-hand woman. And the bossy little sister he'd never had.

When the scandal around Black Crescent had

broken fifteen years ago, and employees as well as friends had abandoned the company and the Lowell family, Haley—a college intern at the time—had remained. Even forgoing a salary to stay. Through the last decade and a half when Joshua had given up his own dreams and passion to step into the gaping, still-hemorrhaging hole his father had left, she'd been loyal. And invaluable. He couldn't have dragged Black Crescent from the brink of financial ruin and rebuilt it without her at his side.

The woman could be a pain in his ass, but she'd proved her loyalty hundreds of times over to his family. Because she was family.

"Since Mom doesn't leave the house too often, I'm not concerned with her mistakenly seeing it," Joshua continued.

Eve had become something of a hermit since her husband's crime and disappearance. Unfortunately, that option hadn't been available to Joshua.

"Good. I don't even want to imagine what this would do to her. Probably send her spiraling into a depression," Oliver said, and while Joshua and his brothers might not agree on much, this one thing they did—their mother's emotional health and protecting her. "I'll go by and see her this evening just to check in."

"That sounds good. Thanks," Joshua replied.

A snort echoed in Joshua's ear. "She's my mother, too. No need to thank me. Talk to you later."

The connection ended, and for a long second, Joshua continued to hold the phone to his ear before lowering it and picking up the newspaper again. He zeroed in on one line that had caught his attention before.

But is Joshua Lowell that different from his father? Appearances, as we know, are often deceiving. Who knows the secrets the Lowell family could still be hiding?

The sentences—no, not so thinly veiled accusations—leaped out at him. What the hell was that supposed to mean? Every skeleton in their closets had been bleached and hung out for everyone to view and tear apart. They didn't have secrets.

And where had she uncovered the photos included in the article? He scrutinized the black-and-white images. A few of his art pieces. His father as he remembered him with his mother on his arm. God, he hadn't seen her smile like that in years. Fifteen of them, to be exact. Him and Jake on their college graduation day, hugging Oliver between them. A family portrait taken at their annual Christmas party. The ones of him and Jake on campus. The snapshots of him painting in art class. The concentration and…joy darkening and lightening his face. He analyzed that image longer, hardly recognizing the young, *hopeful* man in the photo.

Well, Sophie had done her grave-robbing expedition well. He'd accused her of using her shovel to dig up old news. To acquire these photographs, she must've found a fucking backhoe.

Where had she gotten her information? She

shouldn't have had access to those pictures, so who'd provided them to her?

There was only one way to find out.

Joshua tossed the paper to the passenger seat and pressed the ignition button to start the car.

He would go directly to the source.

"Great article, Sophie," Rob Jensen, the entertainment columnist, congratulated with a short rap on the wall of her cubicle.

"Thanks, Rob," she said, smiling. "I appreciate it."

"You did do an excellent job," Marie Coswell added when Rob strode away. She rolled in her desk chair to the edge of her cubicle, directly across from Sophie's. "But wow, woman," she tsk-tsked, shaking her head and sending the blunt edges of her red bob swinging against her jaw. "You didn't hold anything back. Aren't you even the least bit concerned the Lowells will retaliate? I mean, yes, their names were persona non grata around here for a while, but that was a long time ago. They have serious pull and power. Makes me real thankful that I'm over in fashion. No way in hell would I want to tangle with a Lowell, especially Joshua Lowell. Well, hold on. I take that back." She grinned, comically wriggling her perfectly arched eyebrows. "I'd love to tangle with that man—but nekkid."

Sophie laughed at her friend's outrageousness even as heat streamed up her chest and throat and poured into her face. Times like these, she cursed her father's Irish roots. Even her Italian heritage, inherited from her mother, couldn't combat the fair skin that emblazoned every emotion on her face. Good God. She was twenty-eight and blushing like a hormonal teenager.

"Holy shit. Are you blushing, Sophie? At what? The thought of Mr. Tall-Insanely-Rich-and-Hot-as-Hell?" Marie gave an exaggerated gasp. "Oh, you *so* are. All right, give. What happened when you stormed over to his office like it was the Alamo? Did you rip something else besides a strip off his hide? Like his clothes? What aren't you telling me?"

Sophie groaned, closing her eyes at her friend's exuberance and the *volume* of it. She loved the other woman, but she really should've been the gossip editor with her sheer adoration for it.

"Nothing happened. Clothes remained intact. The only thing stripped away was my pride." She winced, just remembering her ill-conceived decision to charge into Joshua Lowell's office and the ensuing confrontation.

That definitely hadn't been one of her finer moments. Thank goodness the front desk receptionist at the main level had been away from her desk. Otherwise security would've probably been called on her. Wouldn't Althea Granger, the editor in chief, have loved to receive that call about one of her investigative reporters needing to be bailed out for trespassing?

Why Joshua hadn't had her escorted out still nagged at her. Just as memories of the CEO did.

She shook her head, as if she could dislodge the question and the man from her mind with the gesture. As if it were that simple.

"Sophie." Althea Granger appeared next to her cubicle, as if her thoughts had conjured the older woman. With thick dark hair, smooth, unlined brown skin and beautiful features, she could've easily been mistaken for a retired model rather than the editor in chief of the exclusive bedroom community of Falling Brook's newspaper. But after stints in major papers across the country, she'd run the *Chronicle* with a steel hand, judicious eye and the political acumen of a seasoned senator for years. And she was Sophie's mentor and idol. "Could you join me in the conference room, please?"

"Absolutely." Sophie rose from her desk chair, ignoring Marie's concerned glance. Too bad she couldn't do the same for the kernel of trepidation that lodged between her ribs. Usually, if Althea wanted to speak with her, it was in her office. Not the more formal conference room.

Could this be about her article? No, it couldn't be. She instantly rejected the thought. Althea had personally read and approved the story before it'd run in this morning's paper. If she'd thought Sophie had gone too far, hadn't been professional or objective in her reporting, the other woman would've had no problem in calling her on it.

Then what could it...possibly...be... *Oh God.*

She almost jolted to a halt in the doorway of the room where most of their editorial meetings were held. Somehow, she managed not to grab on to the jamb to steady her suddenly precarious balance.

Joshua Lowell.

He stood at the head of the long, rectangular table, hands in the pockets of his perfectly tailored, probably ridiculously expensive navy blue suit, those unnervingly sharp and beautiful hazel eyes fixed on her.

How wrong that eyes so lovely—light brown with vivid brushes of emerald green—were wasted on such a hard, cold…gorgeous…face.

Okay. So, she hadn't fabricated how unjustly stunning the man was. It seemed unfair, really. Joshua Lowell, a millionaire, CEO, son of a powerful if notorious family, educated and sophisticated, and then God had deemed fit to top that sundae of privilege with a face and body that belonged pressed on an ancient coin or forever immortalized in marble for some art collector's pleasure.

She tried and failed not to stare at the angular face with its jut of cheekbones and stone-hewn jaw—the stark lines should've been severe, made him appear harsh. But the beauty of those eyes and the lushness of his too-sensual-for-her-comfort mouth with its fuller bottom lip softened the severity, making him a fascinating study of contrasts. Cruelty and tenderness. Coldness and warmth. Carnality and virtue.

Her gaze reluctantly drifted from his face to his broad shoulders, the wide chest that tapered to a narrow waist and hips. She couldn't see his thighs from her still-frozen position in the doorway, but her brain helpfully supplied how the muscular length of them had pressed against his slacks days ago. With his lean but powerful body, the man obviously worked out. Probably unleashed a lot of aggression there.

How else did he release emotion?

Stop it, she snapped at her wayward mind. *We don't care.*

Mentally rolling her eyes at herself, she forced her feet to move forward, carrying her farther into the room. Joshua Lowell might look like he flew down on winged feet from Mount Olympus, but he was still an arrogant ass. One who, most likely, was here either to try to get her fired or threaten a lawsuit. That ought to knock down his hot factor several notches.

Should.

"Sophie, please close the door behind you," Althea instructed. Once Sophie shut the door with a quiet click, the editor in chief nodded toward Joshua. "Mr. Lowell, I'd like to introduce you to Sophie Armstrong, the journalist of the article in today's edition."

Her pulse echoed in her ears as she waited, breath snagged in her throat, for Joshua to out her to her employer. But after a long moment, he only arched a dark blond eyebrow. His gaze didn't waver from her as he smoothly said, "Ms. Armstrong."

Relief flooded her, almost weakening her knees. Above all things, Althea was a professional, and she wouldn't have appreciated finding out Sophie had met him before. No, correction. *How* she'd met him.

But suspicion immediately nipped at relief's heels. *Why* hadn't he told Althea the truth? What did he want? She didn't know him, but she doubted he did anything magnanimously without it benefiting him. And he owed nothing to her, the reporter who had just aired his family's dark past all over the front page.

"Ms. Granger, I would appreciate it if you gave Ms. Armstrong and me a moment alone, please." He'd added *please*, but it wasn't a request.

And Althea didn't take it as one, though she did turn to her and ask, "Sophie?"

No. The answer branded her tongue, but the last time she'd checked, she wasn't a coward. And since she'd crashed Black Crescent's proverbial gates, it would be the height of hypocrisy to claim fear of being alone with him now. Even if her heart thudded against her chest like a bass drum.

"It's fine," she said.

"Okay." She continued to peer at Sophie for several more seconds, and, apparently satisfied with Sophie's poker face, she nodded. "Fine, but, Mr. Lowell," she added, swinging her attention back to Joshua, "I'm going to trust the words *lawsuit* and *libel* won't be thrown around in my absence. If so, I fully advise and expect Sophie to end the conversation so I can introduce you to our legal department."

With a smile that belied she'd just threatened to sic lawyers on him, Althea exited the room, leaving her alone with Joshua. And a table that had provided adequate enough distance before seemed to shrink, leaving her no protection.

"I assume your editor doesn't know about your little excursion to my office," he stated, with that flat note she'd come to associate with him.

"No," she said. "But of course you already figured that out. Why didn't you tell her?"

"Because it doesn't serve me well to do so right

now. And—" his voice deepened to a slightly ominous timbre that had trepidation and—*God*—whispers of excitement tripping down her spine "—if anyone is going to deliver trouble to your doorstep, Sophie Armstrong, it's going to be me."

That statement might not have contained *lawsuit* or *libel*, but it was still most definitely a threat.

"I assume you're here about the piece in the *Chronicle*." She switched the subject, not wanting to dwell on what kind of "trouble" he wanted to visit on her. "Why don't you just get to it?"

He studied her, his silence heavy but fairly vibrating with the tension that seemed to crackle beneath his stoic facade. And something—call it a reporter's instinct or a woman's sixth sense—assured her that it was indeed a facade. Which meant more lurked beneath the surface that he didn't want anyone to see, to know. Secrets. The journalist in her, definitely *not* the woman, wanted to ferret out those secrets. Hungered to expose them to the light.

"Yes, why don't we just 'get to it,'" he repeated, making her suggestion sound like something more wicked. "I want to know how you acquired the photographs in the article."

She crossed her arms over her chest and shook her head. "From my sources, and before you issue a demand wrapped up in a request, I can't reveal them."

"Can't," he pressed, "or won't?"

She shrugged a shoulder. "In this case, it's the same difference."

Another long beat where his unwavering, intense

gaze scrutinized her. "Do you know what you are, Ms. Armstrong?" he finally murmured.

"Let me guess. A bitch," she supplied, slipping a bored note into her voice. Wouldn't be the first time a man in his position had called her that name when she'd pressed too hard, questioned too much or just didn't go sit behind a desk or on a set and look pretty. Journalism, especially investigative journalism, wasn't for the weak of heart or the thin of skin. And that word seemed to be the go-to to describe a strong woman with an opinion, a spine and unwillingness to be silenced.

"No." A flash of disgust flickered across his face as if just hearing that word sickened him. Or maybe the thought of calling a woman that particular insult did… "Maybe you would prefer if I called you that. Because then you could justify my being here as sour grapes and damaged pride over a story. But I refuse to make it that easy for you. No, Ms. Armstrong, you are not a bitch," he continued, and the disdain that had appeared in his expression saturated his voice. "You are a vulture. A scavenger who picks at carrion until there's nothing left but the bleached, dry bones."

That shouldn't have hurt her. But, God, it did. It slashed across her chest to burrow deep beneath bone and marrow to the core of her that believed in fairness and truth. Never in her reporting had she gone out of the way to hurt someone. Which had been one reason why she'd gone to see Joshua in the first place. She'd wanted his side, to ensure the article hadn't been skewed.

Maybe it was a remnant from being the child of divorced parents. From that hyperawareness that ensured neither her mother nor her father feel like she loved one more than the other. That she didn't confide in, call or lavish attention on one without making sure she gave the other equal affection. That balance had been stressful as a child who'd felt torn between two warring parents. And now, as an adult, that careful balancing act had carried over into her job. She ensured she presented both sides of an issue. And for Joshua to attack that vulnerable center of her... It shook her. It *hurt* her.

"In your thirst for a juicy story and a byline, did you even once stop to consider the consequences? Did you pause to ask yourself how it would affect my family? My mother? She's had to deal with the fallout of someone else's actions for years. *Years*," he bit out, true anger melting the ice of his tone. Sunlight streamed through the windows behind him, hitting his dirty-blond hair and setting the gold strands aglow. Like an avenging angel. "She's suffered, and dredging up ancient history for the sake of salacious gossip will only inflict more harm. But, of course, you couldn't be bothered to take into account anyone or anything else but your own ambition."

"My own ambition?" she repeated, grinding the words out between clenched teeth. She lowered her arms and her fingers curled into fists at her thighs, as she almost trembled with the need to defend herself. To tell him that wasn't her at all. But screw that. She hadn't done a hatchet job; she'd simply done her job.

Period. And she'd been fair. *Damn fair.* "You don't know the first thing about me, so don't shove your own biases on me. I understand that you might not be able to view the article objectively, but believe me, I showed admirable restraint. I could have included the complete, unvarnished truth about who and what you are. A truth I'm sure the 'hero'—" she sneered the word "—of Black Crescent wouldn't want to get out."

He didn't reply. Didn't react at all. His hazel gaze bored into her, and she refused to flinch under that poker face that reduced hers to an amateurish attempt.

"I have no idea what you're alluding to. I haven't done anything wrong or that I need to be ashamed of. As much to the contrary as your story hinted at, I haven't been my father's puppet. I've done nothing but try to repair the damage he caused. That's all I've ever done."

Joshua probably wasn't aware of the strained note in his voice, the almost silent fervency that stretched from his words. Yes, she couldn't deny the truth of his statement. Even if the possibility existed that Vernon was pulling the strings all these years, it didn't negate the fact that Joshua had abandoned what had appeared to be a very promising art career to take over the family company. To head it and bear all the heat, enmity and distrust as well as the responsibility on his still-young shoulders. His twin, Jake, hadn't been seen in Falling Brook for fifteen years, and the younger brother, Oliver, had fallen into a destructive partying lifestyle. So everything had fallen to him, and Joshua had put aside his own dreams to take up the burden.

No matter how she felt about the man and his actions, she had to respect that sacrifice.

"Anything I've done, it was and is to protect and take care of my family. I have no shame in that," he said, and that air of arrogance, of utter lack of remorse just… Dammit, it just pissed her off.

"Now, that is rich coming from you," she drawled, propping a hip against the conference table.

His aloof expression remained, but he cocked his head to the side. "And what the hell do you mean by that?" he demanded, almost…pleasantly. But the glitter in his eyes belied the tone.

"Oh, I think you know… *Daddy.*"

He blinked, continuing to stare at her. And his lack of response, of reaction, only stirred the anger kindling in her chest.

"Really?" she snapped. "You're going to continue to pretend to not know what I'm talking about?" She chuckled, the sound brittle, jaded and lacking humor. "You only protect and care for the family you decide to acknowledge. But," she chided, tapping a fingertip to the corner of her mouth, "I suppose that a four-year-old daughter would be extremely inconvenient for someone who lives on that high horse you're so afraid to tumble off of."

Joshua slowly leaned forward and, with a deliberate motion, flattened his palms on the table. "I don't know why you seem to believe that I have a child, but I don't. That's crazy," he said, narrowing his eyes on her.

She snorted. "Just because you might claim you don't—and you definitely act like you don't have a daughter—doesn't make it so."

He didn't reply, but that piercing gaze didn't leave her face. His tall, rangy body remained motionless, coiled as if pulled taut by an invisible string—a string that was seconds from snapping.

She frowned, stepping back from her indignation and, okay, yes, battered pride and feelings, to analyze him more closely. Confusion, and, *oh God*, whispers of uncertainty darkened his eyes.

Could it... *Could he really not know?*

"I—I..." She stopped. Inhaled. And started again. "I'm not making this claim casually or lightly. I have very good reason to believe that you do have a daughter."

"I don't know what your reasons are, and I don't care," he said with the barest hint of a rasp. "And if you knew anything about me beyond your so-called research, you would realize how ridiculous your accusation is. Because that's what you telling me I have a child I've neglected is, Ms. Armstrong. An ugly, unfounded and *untrue* accusation."

She should've flinched at his menacing growl, at the blistering curse. She *should not* be electrified by it. Should not be riveted and fascinated by the sign of heat and a loosening of his iron-clad control.

Should not be considering poking more at the bear, to see if he would roar instead of growl. To see if he would...pounce.

Ill-conceived and unwelcomed desire leaped and cavorted in her veins like a naughty, giggling child. One who didn't care one bit for the rules. She steeled her body against the dark urge to draw nearer to him. Against the almost irresistible need to discover if his body warmth seeped through his suit and see if it would touch her. To find out what scent his skin held. Something earthy and raw, or would it be cool and refined? Fire or ice?

She cleared her throat and inched back, her hip bumping one of the chairs flanking the table. *Jesus, woman. He's not the pied piper, and you aren't some glaze-eyed mouse.* And besides, if she decided to follow any man somewhere—which hell would have to fall into a deep freeze and sell snow cones for extra income for that to happen—it wouldn't be this icicle of a man who carried more baggage than a Boeing 747.

"Listen, I received this information from a source—one that I trust. And if you recall, I attempted to reach out numerous times to interview you for the article. If you had bothered replying to any of my calls, voice mails or emails, I would've addressed this with you. But the fact that you refused only lent credence to my suspicions that you had something to hide." She ignored the scoff he uttered and spread her hands wide, palms up. "I know you doubt my credibility, but I thoroughly researched your family to prepare for my article. And the truth is the rumor about an illegitimate child surfaced several times."

"This source you trust," he countered, "would it be the same one who provided those pictures?"

She hesitated but, after a second, nodded. "Yes."

Of the people she'd interviewed, Zane Patterson had proved to be the most helpful...and rich in information. Rich, hell. He'd been a gold strike. And none of what he'd had to share had been flattering. But considering his family had been one of those directly affected by the Black Crescent scandal, Sophie couldn't blame him for his animosity and bitterness. He'd lost everything—his family's financial security, his home and then his family. His parents had divorced a year later. And he blamed it all on the Lowells. The man still harbored a lot of anger toward that family.

Still, just because he hated them didn't mean he hadn't been able to give her plenty of material. Zane had been a year younger than Oliver Lowell, so they'd run in the same circles in high school. Therefore, he'd had the means to supply her with the kind of info that hadn't been available with a Google search as fifteen years ago social media hadn't been as prevalent as it was today. Not only had Zane given her the photos Joshua seemed so fixated on, but he'd also been the first person to mention Joshua having a love child that he refused to acknowledge. But, like she'd assured Joshua, Zane hadn't been the only person to assert the same.

"Fine. Keep your secrets," Joshua said. He turned away from her, studying the just-awakening main street of Falling Brook. The newspaper's offices were located in one of the older brick buildings lining the street, tucked between a women's clothing boutique and a bookstore. As he stared out the window, the sun's rays caressing his sharply hewn profile, he was like a king surveying his realm.

And maybe he was. The insular bedroom community with its two-thousand-strong population of surgeons, CEOs, a few A-list actors and pro athletes had once looked at Vernon Lowell as a ruler, and Joshua's father had gorged on the admiration and reverence. By all appearances, Joshua seemed to be a more benevolent king, but no one could mistake the power, the air of authority and command that clung to him, as tailor-made to fit as his suits.

Part of her acknowledged she should be intimidated by that level of influence. In this community where money not just spoke, but screamed at the tops of its lungs, power of the press was a buzz phrase. If he wanted, he could have her fired. Blackballed, even.

So yes, she should be at least a little leery. But fear didn't skip and dance over her skin, leaving pebbled flesh in its wake. Exhilaration did. Being in this man's presence agitated and animated her in a way only burgeoning new stories did. And the why of it—she lurched away from digging deeper, scrabbling away from that particular crumbling, dangerous edge.

When he turned back and pinned her with that magnetic, intense gaze, she barely managed to trap her gasp. The force of it was nearly physical. The inane image of her holding her hands up, shielding herself from it, popped in her head.

"You're right," he announced.

She blinked, taken aback. Replaying their conversation through her mind, she shook her head, still confused. "About?"

"You offered me the opportunity to give my insight into the story, and I didn't take it. But now I'm offering you a chance no other reporter has been extended. Come spend a day with me at the Black Crescent offices. I'll grant you access to my world, and you can see and decide for yourself whether or not the rumors stated in your article are true. Or you might just discover that I'm just a businessman trying to repair the past while making a way for the future." He arched an eyebrow. "Either way, it will be an exclusive."

It's a trap. The warning blared through her head. And if she had the intelligence God gave a gnat, she would decline. But she was aware enough to recognize that the woman whispered that caution. The reporter's blood hummed with anticipation at this unprecedented opportunity. She could pen a part two to her piece, and maybe it and the first one could possibly be picked up by the *Associated Press*.

Plus you get to spend more time with Joshua Lowell. The sly whisper ghosted across her mind. Spend more time with the enigmatic, sexy man who kindled a need inside her that she resented. A need that, if she wasn't careful, could compromise her objectivity and her job.

And that she absolutely couldn't allow. Nothing could get in the way of her goals, of her independence. Her mother had shelved her dream of becoming an architect to marry her father. And years later, when her marriage ended, she'd had to start from scratch, dependent on the scant alimony her father had grudgingly provided, having to work low-paying jobs to make ends meet while attending college part-time. It'd taken years of dedication and exhausting, back-breaking work, but she'd finally attained her dream job. But Sophie had learned a valuable lesson while witnessing her mother's struggle. She would never become a casualty of a relationship. And never would she prioritize a man above her own needs, giving him everything while he left her with just scraps to remind her of what she could've had but had thrown away.

She had to take only one look at Joshua Lowell, spend one minute in his company, take one glance in those lovely but shuttered eyes to know he could strip her of everything. And not look back.

If she allowed him to. Which she wouldn't.

"I accept your offer," she said, resolve strengthening her voice.

He dipped his head in acknowledgment. "I'll have my assistant contact you to set up an appointment."

With one last, long stare, he strode toward her, heading toward the conference room door. As he brushed past her, she ordered herself not to inhale. Not to find out—

Sandalwood and dark earth after a fresh spring rain. Earthy and raw, it is.

Dammit.

"Ms. Armstrong." She jerked her head in his direction and met the gaze of the ruthless businessman who had dragged a failing company back from the edge of the financial abyss. "Don't mistake this for an olive branch or a truce. When you wrote and published that article, you threatened the peace and well-being of my family, and I don't take that lightly or forget. Use this as a chance for another smear campaign, and I'll ensure you regret it."

Long after he left, his warning—and his scent—remained.

No matter how hard she tried to eradicate both.

Three

Joshua pulled his car into the parking lot of his gym and stabbed the ignition button a little harder than necessary, shutting the engine off. Restless energy raced through him, and it jangled under his skin. He'd been this way since yesterday and his visit to the *Falling Brook Chronicle*'s offices. Since his confrontation with Sophie.

Tunneling his fingers through his hair, he gripped the short strands and ground his teeth together. Trapping the searing flood of curses that blistered his tongue. He'd gone there to question her about the photographs and her source for them. And he'd been slapped with a paternity accusation.

The *fuck*.

Even now icy fingers of shock continued to tickle

his spine, chilling him. Trailing right behind it came the hot slam of helpless fury. He hated that sense of powerlessness, of—goddammit—self-doubt.

And he resented the hell out of Sophie for planting it there. For hauling him back to a time when he'd been drowning in fear, desperately swimming toward the surface to drag in a life-giving lungful of air. Despairing that he never would again.

Through the years, there'd been plenty of gossip about his family on top of the ugly truth about his father and his actions. It would be a lie to claim the whispers hadn't hurt him. That he didn't have scars from that tumultuous period. But he'd survived. He'd always had pride in the knowledge that he wasn't his father, that he didn't harm people out of selfishness and greed. He'd clung to that knowledge.

And in one conversation, Sophie had delivered a solid blow to that source of honor, causing zigzags to splinter through it like a cracked windshield.

Had he been a monk? Hell no. He enjoyed sex, but he still practiced caution. A man in his position and with his wealth had to. So he chose his partners carefully—women who understood he didn't want a relationship, just a temporary arrangement that provided pleasure for both of them—and ensured he used protection. Still, he understood that mistakes could happen. Nothing was infallible. But none of his ex-lovers had ever approached him about an unexpected pregnancy or a child. Because if they had, he would've never abandoned the woman or the baby. *Never.*

For Sophie to suggest—no, to accuse him of being able to neglect his own flesh and blood...

With a low growl, he shoved open his car door and stepped out, slamming it shut behind him. Seconds later, with his duffel bag in hand, he stalked toward the gym, ready to work off some of the anger and tension riding him like a relentless jockey on a punching bag.

An hour later, sweat poured from his face, shoulders and chest in rivulets. Pleasurable weariness born of pushing his body to the limit sang in his muscles. Yanking off his boxing gloves, he picked up his bottle of water and gulped it while inhaling the scent of perspiration, bleach and the musk from bodies that had permanently seeped into the concrete floors and walls. This gym, located in the next town over from Falling Brook, wasn't one of those trendy establishments soccer moms and young CEOs patronized with stylish athletic wear and skin that glistened or, for God's sake, *dewed.*

Fighters grappled and trained in the boxing ring at the far side of the room. Huge tires leaned against a wall and a smattering of paint-flecked, scratched gym equipment hogged one corner while free weights claimed another. Grunts, the smack of rope hitting the concrete floor and rock music permeated the air. People didn't come to this to be seen, but to push their bodies, to beat them into submission or perfect working order.

So what the *fuck* was Sophie Armstrong doing here?

He scowled, studying the petite, frowning woman as she whipped the battle ropes up and down in a steady, furious pace. Even as the familiar anger and suspicion crowded into him at the sight of her in the gym he'd frequented for years—his sanctuary away from the office and home—he couldn't stop his gaze from following the slender but toned lines of her small frame that the purple sports bra and black leggings did nothing to hide. Without the conservative clothes that halted just shy of being plain, he had an unrestricted view of the high thrust of her smallish and utterly perfect breasts that slightly swelled over the rounded edge of her top. Though he ordered himself to look away, to stop visually devouring the enemy, he still lingered over the taut abdomen that gleamed with hard-fought-for sweat and the gently rounded hips and tight, sleekly muscled legs that seemed impossibly long for someone of her stature.

Like a sweaty elf princess who'd momentarily traded her gilded throne for a dusty battlefield. The silly, fanciful thought swept through his head before he could banish it. Thoughts like that belonged to the artist he used to be, not the sensible, pragmatic businessman he was now. Still… Watching her muscles flex, her abs tighten and those strong thighs brace her weight, he was impressed at the power in her tiny frame.

Impressed and hard as hell.

"Goddamn," he growled. Frolicking puppies. Spreadsheets with unbalanced columns.

His mother's shuttered face and devastated eyes when she read Sophie's article.

Yeah, that killed his erection fast.

And maybe it didn't snuff out the hot licks of lust in his gut, but it gave fury one hell of a foothold.

Clenching his jaw, he stalked across the gym toward the woman who had infiltrated his life and cracked open a door he'd hoped, fucking prayed, would remain locked, bolted and welded shut. Just as he reached Sophie, she gave the battle ropes one last flick, then dropped them to the floor with a thud.

"Stalking me, Ms. Armstrong?" he drawled, his fingers gripping his water bottle so tight, the plastic squeaked in protest.

He immediately loosened his hold. Damn, he'd learned long ago to never betray any weakness of emotion. People were like sharks scenting bloody chum in the water when they sensed a chink in his armor. But when in this woman's presence, his emotions seemed to leak through like a sieve. The impenetrable shield barricading him that had been forged in the fires of pain, loss and humiliation came away dented and scratched after an encounter with Sophie. And that presented as much of a threat, a danger to him as her insatiable need to prove that he was a deadbeat father and puppet to a master thief.

"Stalking you?" she scoffed, bending down to swipe her own bottle of water and a towel off the ground. With a strength that could be described only as Herculean, he didn't drop his gaze to the sweet, firm curve of her ass. He deserved a medal, an award, the key to the city for not giving in to the urge. "Need I remind you, it was you who showed up at my job yesterday, not the other way around. So I guess that makes us even in the showing-up-where-we're-not-wanted department."

"Oh, we're not even close to anything that resembles *even*, Sophie," he said, using her name for the first time aloud. And damn if it didn't taste good on his tongue. If he didn't sound as if he were stroking the two syllables like they were bare, damp flesh.

She didn't immediately reply, instead lifting the clear bottle to her mouth and sipping from it. His gaze dipped to that pursed, wicked mouth, and a primal throb set up in his blood, his dick. *Stand down*, he ordered his unruly flesh. His loose gray basketball shorts wouldn't conceal the effect she had on him. And no way in hell would he give her that to use against him.

"I hate to disappoint you and your dreams of narcissistic grandeur, but I've been a member of this gym for years." She swiped her towel over her throat and upper chest. "I've seen you here, but it's not my fault if you've never noticed me."

"That's bullshit," he snapped. "I would've noticed you."

The words echoed between them, the meaning in them pulsing like a thick, heavy heartbeat in the sudden silence that cocooned them. Her silver eyes flared wide before they flashed with...what? Surprise? Irritation? Desire. A liquid slide of lust prowled through him like a hungry—so goddamn hungry—beast.

The air simmered around them. How could no one else see it shimmer in waves from the concrete floor like steam from a sidewalk after a summer storm?

She was the first to break the visual connection, and when she ducked her head to pat her arms down, the loss of her eyes reverberated in his chest like a physical snapping of tautly strung wire. He fisted his fingers at his sides, refusing to rub the echo of soreness there.

"Do you want me to pull out my membership card to prove that I'm not some kind of stalker?" She tilted her head to the side. "I'm dedicated to my job, but I refuse to cross the line into creepy...or criminal."

He ground his teeth against the apology that shoved at his throat, but after a moment, he jerked his head down in an abrupt nod. "I'm sorry. I shouldn't have jumped to conclusions." And then because he couldn't resist, because it still gnawed at him when he shouldn't have cared what she—a reporter—thought of him or not, he added, "That predilection seems to be in the air."

She narrowed her eyes on him, and a tiny muscle ticked along her delicate but stubborn jaw. Why that sign of temper and forced control fascinated him, he opted not to dwell on. "And what is that supposed to mean?" she asked, the pleasant tone belied by the anger brewing in her eyes like gray storm clouds.

Moments earlier, he'd wondered if fury or desire had heated her gaze. Now he had his answer. Because he now faced her anger, now had confirmation that when she looked like she wanted to knee him in the balls the silver darkened to near black.

But when she looked like she just wanted to go

to her knees for him, her eyes were molten, pure hot silver.

God help him, because, masochistic fool that he'd suddenly become, he craved them both.

He wanted her rage, her passion...wanted both to beat at him, heat his skin, touch him. Make him feel.

Mentally, he scrambled away from that, that *need*, like it'd reared up and flashed its fangs at him. The other man he'd been—the man who'd lost himself in passion, paint and life captured on film—had drowned in emotion. Willingly. Joyfully. And when it'd been snatched away—when that passion, that *life*—had been stolen from him by cold, brutal reality, he'd nearly crumbled under the loss, the darkness. Hunger, wanting something so desperately, led only to the pain of eventually losing it.

He'd survived that loss once. Even though it'd been like sawing off his own limbs. He might be an emotional amputee, but dammit, he'd endured. He'd saved his family, their reputation and their business. But he'd managed it by never allowing himself to need again.

And Sophie Armstrong, with her pixie face and warrior spirit, wouldn't undo all that he'd fought and silently screamed to build.

She must've interpreted his silence as an indictment, because her full mouth firmed into an aggravated line, and her shoulders slowly straightened, her posture militant and, yes, defensive. As she should be. "If it makes it easier to look at that pretty face in the mirror, then go ahead and throw verbal punches," she sneered. *Pretty face.* He didn't even pretend to take that for a compliment. Not that way her voice twisted around the words. "But I did the research, and the information I received was solid, and my sources were legitimate."

"Sources," he repeated, leaping on that clue. "So you had more than one?"

She didn't move, but she might as well as have slammed up an invisible door between them. "Yes," she replied after a long moment. "I didn't rely on gossip or groundless rumors."

"Your sources seem to believe they know a lot about not just my family, the inner workings of Black Crescent, but my personal life, as well," he said, drawing closer to her.

The seeds that their earlier conversation in the *Chronicle*'s conference room had planted started to sprout roots. Roots of suspicion and hated mistrust wound their way into his head, threading around his heart. He resented Sophie for planting those kernels of suspicion about the people who existed in his small inner circle. Small for a reason. Trial by fire had taught him he could trust a precious few, and only those precious few had access to his family, the details of his life. Could one of them be the "source" she referred to? As he'd done on the drive back to his office yesterday, he again ran through their faces: Haley, Jake, Oliver.

Haley, no. Never. She'd proved her loyalty hundreds of times over. But his brothers... Jesus, he wanted to dismiss any notion that they could've turned on him, but… He couldn't. They resented him, resented that he'd become their father, never appreciating the sacrifices he'd made so they could live free of the burden of Black Crescent and the dark shadow it cast. A shadow he constantly existed in but strove to, if not be free of, at least lighten.

"I want names, Sophie," he bit out, the dregs of fear, grief and anger at the possible identities of her sources swirling in his mind roughening his voice. He stepped closer until the scent of citrus, velvet, damp blooms and woman—*her*—filled his nostrils. Ignoring the lure of that sensual musk, he lowered his head, forcing her to meet his gaze. "If someone is digging into my life and giving information about me, then I deserve to know who they are." *Who I need to protect myself from.* "Every man has the right to confront their accusers."

She shook her head, her golden-brown ponytail brushing her bare shoulders. "No. The people who spoke to me did so on the assurance of confidentiality, and I won't betray that. And I absolutely refuse to expose them to the wrath of the Lowell family."

The wrath of the Lowell family? What kind of shit was that? "My wrath?" he murmured, edging closer. And closer still until one shift of his feet and their chests would press together. Their sweat-dampened skin would cling. His cock would find a home nestled against her taut stomach. "Do you still have your job? Have you found yourself and that paper you work for served with a defamation suit? If you went to any of the stores or restaurants around here, would you still be waited on or served? No, Sophie." He leaned down, so close his lips almost grazed her ear. So close, he caught the shiver that worked through her body as his breath hit her lobe. "If I wanted to wage war against someone who came after me, after mine, the first casualty would be you. And since you haven't been shunned or blackballed yet—because believe me, even with the stain on my last name, I have the power to do all I've mentioned—you haven't felt my wrath. Besides," he added, and this time he let his mouth brush the rim of her ear. Let himself get his first feel of her skin, her body even if it was just something as small as that. "I would never include others in the battle between us. This, sweetheart, is personal."

Air, quick and harsh, rushed from her lips, bathing his cheek, stirring the flames already stroking him from the inside out. God, he wanted to… Grinding his molars together so hard he should've tasted dust, he inched back, placing between them the space he'd so foolishly eliminated. As it was, he now fought the impulse to rub his thumb over the spot where his mouth had glanced her ear. Rub that sensation into his flesh as if it wasn't already branded there.

"Is that supposed to scare me? Should I file that under the threat category?" she shot back. And it would've been effective if it hadn't been uttered in a throaty whisper that rasped over his too-sensitive skin.

Damn her.

Damn him.

"No, Sophie. The last thing I want from you is fear." Let her translate that how she wanted. "But make no mistake, I intend to have those names from you. And that's not a threat, but a promise."

Not waiting for her response, he turned and strode away from her. But not for long. They had an appointment for a day together at his office. And he would see the vow he'd made come true.

Sophie would divulge the identities of her sources.

One way or another.

And as his blood hummed in his veins, still lit up like a torch from his interaction with her, it was the "another" that worried him.

Four

Back in the lion's den.

Sophie summoned a smile as she gave the first-floor receptionist of the Black Crescent building her name and waited while she called to verify her appointment. Turning, she stared at the large picture window, not really seeing the parking lot or the ring of towering trees beyond that shielded the property like an inner wall in a medieval fiefdom.

No, images of Joshua Lowell from when he'd cornered her at the gym yesterday flickered before her eyes. Flickered, hell. Paraded. Him, his lean but large and powerful body encased in a sweaty white T-shirt that clung to tendon and muscle, and loose gray knee-length basketball shorts. God, those shorts. If the shirt had her itching to climb those wide shoulders as if they were a scratching post and she was a cat in heat, then those shorts had her palm itching to slide beneath the damp waistband, skim over his ridged abdomen and farther down to grasp the long and thick length that she'd glimpsed the imprint of under the nylon.

Joshua freaking Lowell had been hard. *For her.*

And he'd called her sweetheart.

She still couldn't wrap her mind around that. He hated her. Okay, *hate* might be too strong a word, but he very strongly disliked her. Okay, *disliked* might be too soft a word.

Sighing, she shook her head, dispelling the mental picture, but could do nothing for the sensitive spot just under her navel. The spot where his cock had pressed against her as he'd whispered threats—forget *promises*, those had definitely been *threats*—in her ear. Idiot that she was, she should've been furious, or even a little intimidated, but no.

She'd just been turned the hell on.

And all she could think of was whether or not that sandalwood, earth and rain scent would transfer to her skin if his naked, big body covered hers. Would she wear him on her? Or would they create a new fragrance together—one made of him, her and sex?

Stop this. Now. The silent but strident admonishment rang inside her head, and she heeded it. She *had* to. In several very short minutes, she would once again face Joshua on his turf. Only this time she wouldn't have the benefit of surprise. He would have home-court advantage, so to speak, prepared for her, her questions, her preconceived perceptions of him. Joshua Lowell would be ready to battle. And as he'd warned her, he wouldn't lose.

She had to be focused and professional and, above all, could not think of how that beautiful body would feel moving over her...in her.

Dammit!

"Ms. Armstrong, they're expecting you upstairs. If you'll take the elevator to the second floor, Mr. Lowell's executive assistant, Haley Shaw, will be waiting for you." The woman gave her a polite but friendly smile as she gestured toward the bank of elevators that Sophie was all too familiar with. She'd covertly stole into them to barge into the Black Crescent offices to interview Joshua Lowell.

"Thank you," she murmured, and followed the receptionist's directions.

Moments later, she stepped out onto the executive floor and approached Haley Shaw's large circular desk. The pretty blonde stood in front of it, smiling up at a tall, handsome man with light brown hair and a presence that screamed confidence and an intensity he couldn't mask. It was that intensity that had Sophie frowning slightly as she approached the couple.

Though both of their voices contained a light note of flirtation, and Haley didn't appear uncomfortable, the man seemed to invade the other woman's personal space, dwarfing Haley's not-inconsiderable height. As a woman who'd often encountered inappropriate advances in the workplace, maybe Sophie was extra sensitive, but it didn't stop her from nearing them and stopping at the executive assistant's side, facing the man, whose smile widened to include her.

Yeah, she didn't trust that smile at all.

In her experience, people who grinned that wide and tried hard to appear affable were usually hiding something. Using overt friendliness and charm as a deflection.

Something whispered to her that this guy was no different.

"Good morning, Ms. Armstrong," Haley greeted Sophie, surprising her a little with the warmth emanating from the welcome. The last time Sophie had been here, she hadn't made such a good first impression. "Can I introduce you to Chase Hargrove?"

"Mr. Hargrove." Sophie nodded, and he extended his hand toward her.

"Ms. Armstrong. It's a pleasure to meet you." Giving her another of those too-amicable smiles, he switched his attention back to Haley. "I have to go. I'll talk to you later, Haley. Hopefully see you then, too, beautiful." With a wink and crooked grin that even Sophie had to admit had her wanting to fan herself, he turned and strode toward the elevators.

"Wow," Sophie muttered as soon as the doors slid closed behind him. "He's definitely...not shy." She shook her head, huffing out a laugh. "Were you okay with how strong he seemed to be coming on? If not, you should tell—" *Joshua* hovered on her tongue, but after a brief hesitation, she said, "Mr. Lowell."

She scoffed, waving a hand toward the direction Chase had disappeared. "He's harmless. Believe me,

I can handle him." Pushing off the desk, she swept a hand toward the double doors that led to Joshua's office. "He's waiting for you. Did you need anything? Coffee, tea, water?"

"I'm fine, thanks." Sophie would die on the hill of denial before admitting it aloud, but her stomach twisted with nerves and wouldn't be able to handle anything on it.

Haley nodded, and when they approached the door, she gave it a swift knock, then opened it. "Joshua, Ms. Armstrong is here."

Sweat dotted Sophie's palms, and her heart rapped against her sternum, but she managed a smile of thanks and shored up her mental shields as she moved into the office. After his visit to the *Chronicle* and their impromptu meeting at the gym, she didn't even try to delude herself into believing she could prepare herself for coming face-to-face with him again and not be slammed with the intense presence that was Joshua Lowell.

So when he rose from behind his desk, exposing that tall, rangy body to her, she just let herself soak him in. Took in the short, dark blond hair that emphasized the clean but sharp facial features. Met the green-and-light-brown gaze that seemed determined to strip her of all her defenses. Traced the wide, soft-looking mouth with its too-tempting, full bottom lip. Wandered over the muscular strength and animal magnetism that his steel-gray suit accentuated rather than hid in a cloak of civility.

Maybe not resisting the magnetic pull of his utter

sexiness but rather immersing herself in it would strengthen her immunity.

Like a freaking flu shot.

"Sophie," he said, rounding the desk with a confident and commanding stride that shouldn't have set her pulse pounding. But God, did it. "I'm glad you could make it."

She arched an eyebrow. "You doubted I would?"

He halted several feet from her. And it reminded her of how close he'd been in the gym. How his scent had engulfed her. How his lips had brushed her ear even as he whispered threats into it. No. Not threats. Promises, he'd assured her.

And how sick did it make her that a part of her wanted him to follow through on them?

Very. Any therapist worth her or his degree would rub their hands in glee at the thought of getting their hands on her.

"Not for a second," he murmured, that gaze skimming over her emerald sheath and nude pumps before returning to her face.

Her skin hummed from the visual contact, and she fought not to rub her palms up and down her bare arms. She wouldn't give him the satisfaction of knowing he affected her.

"Well, thank you again for the opportunity to tour the inner sanctum of Black Crescent Hedge Fund." See? She could be professional around him. "I'm looking forward to this."

He nodded. "If you'll follow me…"

For the next several hours, Joshua granted her an

exclusive peek behind the curtain. Not only did he introduce her to his employees and explain what they did, but he also revealed how he'd implemented safeguards and a checks-and-balances system so what'd occurred with his father didn't happen again. In other words, he'd willingly policed himself.

She discovered a side of the company she hadn't known existed. Over the years, Joshua had donated a mind-boggling amount of money and time to local and statewide programs that assisted domestic abuse victims, literacy and the foster-care system, including his assistant Haley Shaw's own nonprofit organization. But not only did he help his community, he also invested in his own employees' futures by helping put the staff and their families through college with scholarships and almost-zero-interest loans.

And then there were the reparations he'd made to the families affected by his father's crimes. Joshua had made good on that agreement to repay the stolen funds.

By the time she followed him back to his office that afternoon, she was convinced Black Crescent wasn't the coldhearted, corrupt organization portrayed in the news and even by some of her sources.

By her.

"What you've done here is remarkable," she said as he closed the office door behind them. She shook her head. "Especially in the last few years. But I've only heard of maybe two of your philanthropic efforts. Why haven't you shared with the public what you've shown me today? I think most people would be amazed and as impressed as I am with all that you do for the community on a local and even national level."

"If someone brags about what should be their privilege and right to do, I question not just their motivations but their hearts. Besides—" he slipped his hands into the front pockets of his pants and a faint smile quirked the corners of his mouth "—I've found that most people, particularly the press, have never been interested in reporting anything positive about my family or the company."

She tried not to wince. And didn't quite manage it. "Touché. But to be fair, my article didn't attack you, personally."

"Fair?" he repeated, sarcasm hardening his voice. "Forgive me if I've never associated *fair* with the media. And attack? No. But for an article that was supposed to be about the so-called anniversary of the Black Crescent incident, you invaded my personal life in a way that seemed intrusive and unnecessary."

Her chin snapped up and her shoulders back, offended. "Am I supposed to apologize for being good at my job? I can't control what my sources tell me or where my investigation carries me. I *won't* apologize for the truth. Ever." She narrowed her eyes on him. "If anything you should be thanking me for not including the truth about your illegitimate daughter in the article. I can't say the same would've happened if—"

"Don't say it again," he barked. No, growled. And the ominous rumble of it snapped off her words like a branch cracking from a tree. Thunder rolled across his face, shadowing his eyes and pulling the skin taut across his cheekbones. He took a step forward but drew up short the next instant. "I am. Not. My. Father," he snarled. And somehow, that low, dark statement stunned her more than if he'd yelled it at her. "I would never, ever turn my back on my family the way that bas—"

He broke off, but the rest of his sentence might as well as have been shouted in the room, it echoed so loud, momentarily deafening her.

"The way your father did," she whispered, the words rasping her throat.

Joshua's face could've been carved from stone, but his eyes. God, his eyes damn near glowed with fury…and pain. Such deep, bright pain that the breath caught in her throat, and she ached with it. Ached for him.

She crossed her arms over her chest and turned away from him, eyes momentarily closing. Until this moment Vernon Lowell had been a story, a shadowy, almost urban legend–like figure who'd committed an infamous crime, then disappeared into thin air. But now, in his son's eyes, she saw him as a father—a father who had abandoned and hurt his son so deeply with his actions that even years later, that son suffered. Suffered in ways he hid so successfully that no one—least of all Sophie—had suspected.

That emotion—the intensity of it—couldn't be faked. So was Joshua telling the truth about the child? Did he really not know of her existence? Not only did she rely on her investigative skills in her job, but her instincts. And they were screaming like a pissed-off banshee that maybe, just maybe, he didn't.

Pinching the bridge of her nose, she bowed her head. *I can't believe I'm doing this.* But her heart had made the decision seconds before her brain caught on. And she moved toward the laptop bag she'd left on the couch in the sitting area of his office before leaving for the tour of the company.

Moments later, she had her computer removed and booting up on the coffee table. Glancing up at a still stoic and silent Joshua, she waved him over. "I have something to show you, Joshua," she murmured, using his name for the first time. Something had shifted inside her with that glimpse into his eyes. Standing on formality seemed silly now.

After a brief hesitation, he strode over and lowered onto the cushion next to her. Resolutely attempting to ignore the heat that seemed to emanate from his big body, she focused on pulling up a password-protected file. In several clicks, a report filled the screen.

A DNA report.

He stiffened next to her, and his gaze jerked to her. Silence throbbed in the office, as loud as a heartbeat, as he stared at her. She met his penetrating study evenly, not betraying the wild pounding of her pulse in her ears or the sudden case of dryness that had assaulted her mouth. She couldn't swallow, couldn't move. Common sense railed that she was making a huge mistake, maybe even violating her ethics. But her sense of decency—her soul—insisted that if she could somehow make this right, she should. If she could ease the pain that he would probably deny even existed, she needed to. Whether that was by confirming his daughter's existence or even having a hand in reuniting them... She didn't know. But she had to try.

He turned to her laptop and, leaning forward, scrutinized the report. Taking in his name at the top and the mother's name, which was blacked out. Scanning the results that ended in one determination: Joshua Lowell was a match for a baby girl born four years ago.

Slowly, he straightened. Shock dulled his eyes, flattened the lush curves of his mouth. Only his fists, clenched so tight the knuckles bleached white, betrayed the hint of a stronger current of emotion that could be coursing through him.

Finally, he shifted his gaze to her. "Where did you get this?" he asked, his deep voice like churned-up gravel. It scraped over her skin, abrading her. "Who sent it to you?"

"I can't tell you that."

"Goddammit, Sophie," he snapped. "How can you show me this and then deny me the resources to determine whether it's true or not. Real or not?" he demanded, fury sparking his eyes.

"I can't, Joshua," she insisted. Shaking her head, she spread her hands wide, palms up, on her thighs. "I wish I could, but I *can't*. I will tell you this, though. I believe the report is authentic. My source... I've held the actual report in my hand. If it's faked, it's a fabulous forgery."

"Dammit." He surged off the couch and stalked across the floor to the floor-to-ceiling window that made up one of the walls of his office. Thrusting the

fingers of both hands through his short hair, he uttered a soft "dammit" again, then pressed a fist to the glass and cupped the back of his neck with the other. "How would they even be able to run a DNA test? I've never been asked or consented to giving a sample." He whirled around, his sharp features drawn, taut. "This doesn't make sense. Someone is playing games. They have an endgame that I don't know about and can't figure out."

Sophie stood and ventured a couple of steps in his direction. But didn't travel farther than those steps. Those pinpricks of caution that she'd felt in his presence before now stabbed at her. Warning her to. Back. Off. To retreat and regroup. Because at some point, she'd become too vulnerable to him. Too open.

And that should have her snatching up her belongings and running for the door like he'd just sprouted fur and fangs. Because in her position, vulnerability was a liability. For her and her job. God, she'd already revealed some of her research to him. What next? Ignore a lead? Refuse a story?

End her career?

She'd seen it with her mother.

She'd *been* her mother.

Shame, glittering bright and filthy at the same time, slicked through her like an oil stain. One would think she'd learned her lesson. Because it'd been brutal, but a good one. But those were the best. Or at least, they should be.

Bumping into Laurence Danvers at a local campaign rally four years ago had been an accident, so she'd believed for a long time. She hadn't known then that he'd planned the meeting that had seemed serendipitous. Fated. And she'd fallen so hard for his handsome features, his wide smile, his charm...his lies. She'd allowed her heart to blind her to his true nature. So when he'd first suggested a different perspective on an article she was writing about the city council election candidates, she saw it as his helping her see a different angle. When he'd convinced her that reporting an indiscretion from a candidate's past would be inflammatory and unfair—even though that candidate was running on a family platform—she'd conceded because he was only looking out for her career and reputation as a reputable reporter.

And when he'd demanded that she resign rather than reveal this same candidate had been accused of sexual misconduct by several women, she almost conceded. Almost. Too many times during her relationship with Laurence, she'd ignored her intuition. But that time, she'd listened, done some digging and uncovered that he was a longtime family friend to the candidate whose rally they'd met at. Meeting her, seducing her, making her fall in love... It'd all been so calculated in an effort to use her.

In mere months, she'd almost thrown aside her career, her dreams, her integrity for a man. As Laurence had walked out her apartment door for the final time, she vowed never to be that vulnerable, that *foolish* again.

And as she stared at Joshua, she could feel herself already climbing that slippery slope. One misstep, and it would be a long, painful slide down. Hell, she'd already shown him part of her research. She shuffled back and away from him, both physically and mentally. She had to approach Joshua and this element of her story as a journalist, not a woman who wanted to cradle that strong jaw and massage away the deep crease between his eyebrows. Or soothe the confusion, anger and pain in his eyes.

"Someone is setting me up," Joshua continued, dropping his gaze to his clenched fist. As if disturbed by the outward display of emotion, he stretched his fingers out, splaying them wide and lowering them to the side of his thigh. "Nothing else makes sense. No one has contacted me about possible paternity or approached me for money. Not even threatened blackmail. Logic says that if there was a woman out there with a child I fathered, she would reach out to me for child support."

Sophie couldn't argue with his assumption. Joshua Lowell wasn't only a beautiful man; he was obscenely wealthy and very well connected, even in spite of the scandal. He could more than afford to provide for a child. And a particular kind of woman would use the situation to her advantage and try for more than money. Like forcing a relationship, marriage. Through her research for her article, she'd discovered that from the moment his father disappeared, Joshua had become a choirboy—well, if choirboys had the bodies and faces of Greek gods and exuded sex like a pheromone. But no hint of impropriety had ever been connected to his name in the media. A person didn't need to have a psychology degree to determine the reason behind that. And a woman looking to permanently bind herself to a powerful and rich family would realize that bit of information, as well.

She tapped a finger against her bottom lip. "That is…curious. Especially since the child is four years old now." This was her cue to walk away. To pack up her things, thank him for the opportunity to see the inside of Black Crescent and leave. "I can't give up my sources. But…if you need or want the help, I'll assist in finding out what's going on. Or try to."

Damn.

So much for walking away.

Joshua stared at her for so long, his eyes shuttered, his stony expression indecipherable, that the rescission of her offer hopped on the tip of her tongue. But as she parted her lips, he asked, "Will what you find out end up in the *Chronicle*?"

She extinguished the bright flash of irritation and offense that flared in her chest. Part of her understood his caution and suspicion. But the other half… "I'm not offering my help as part of some tell-all article," she ground out.

God, he really didn't think too much of her.

Which was fair because she didn't trust him, either. From her experience, most men—especially those with something to lose—did everything in their power to protect themselves.

Several more taut seconds passed, but Joshua finally dipped his head in a short, abrupt nod. "I appreciate your offer, then. If there's even the slightest chance that I could be a father, then I owe it to myself—and that little girl—to find out."

A rush of warmth flooded her.

Those aren't the words of a deadbeat father.

Her subconscious taunted like the know-it-all it was.

But her experience with Laurence had hammered home the truth that nothing—or no one—was as it appeared on the surface. Especially someone who had so much to lose like Joshua did—reputation, money and the added burden of a child. Though he managed to keep his private life more contained than others in his position, she'd still gathered images of him and gossip about him with socialites, some A-list actresses and businesswomen.

No middle-class, student-debt-ridden peasants. In other words, no one like you.

Oh, shut it.

Awesome. Now she was arguing with herself. She really needed to get the hell out of this office. This building. This side of town. The more space between her and Joshua right now, the better. If not, she might do something really inane and unforgivable. Like hug him.

Suddenly wary of herself, she turned, retracing the few steps back to the coffee table and couch. Clearing her throat, she sank to the cushion and, tucking a rebellious strand of hair behind her ear, closed her laptop. "I'll start looking into it on my end tonight." With hurried movements, she slid the computer into her bag and stood. Fixing a smile on her lips, she lifted her head and met his impenetrable gaze again. God, the man could give the Sphinx lessons in stoicism. "Thank you for the tour today. I really appreciate it, and I learned more about Black Crescent that I didn't know. That I'm sure many people aren't aware of. If I have your permission, I'd like to share the information in a follow-up article."

"Why?"

She frowned, stilling midprocess of slipping the strap of her bag over her shoulder. "Because the public deserves to know about your philanthropic programs and generosity to the community. I get your reason for staying mum on the subject, but—"

"No." He cut her off with a hard shake of his head. "When I invited you here I knew it was for a follow-up article. I meant why are you volunteering to help me?"

Because you looked so lost, and I want to bring home what will make you whole.

The explanation lodged in her throat, stuck. And she didn't try to free it. One, he wouldn't appreciate her reason. Wouldn't believe her. Two, she was disgusted with herself for thinking it. For thinking she could give him anything, much less peace and comfort.

Yes, Joshua Lowell had the whole brooding, tortured millionaire thing down pat. His cold mask of reserve had slipped enough times that she glimpsed the dark mass of emotions he concealed. She shivered, unable to restrain the telltale reaction. What would it be like to be on the receiving end of all that unleashed passion? Because she sensed that when or if he finally let it all loose… It would be a thing of wild, raw beauty to witness. Like a roiling, ominous thunderstorm threaded with lightning. And when those bolts struck the earth? Electricity, heat, smoke.

Her pulse thundered in her ears, and she couldn't tear her gaze away from him. She couldn't deny it; she hungered to be that rich, open earth electrified by him. But he would assuredly leave her scorched beyond recognition afterward. And while her body might crave that burning, her scarred heart feared it.

Inhaling a trembling breath past the constriction blocking her throat, she shrugged a shoulder, grabbing for nonchalance and praying she accomplished it. "Because I'm an investigative reporter, and that's what I do. Investigate." Hiking her purse strap up, she again curved her lips into a polite smile that she— please, God—hoped didn't look as fake as it felt. "I need to head out so I can get back in the office to take care of a few things." Dear Lord, she was babbling and couldn't stop. "Thanks again, and I'll be in touch."

Crossing the room, she extended her hand toward him even though her mind screamed, *What the hell are you doing? Don't touch him!*

But her body had a mind of its own. And as his strong, elegant fingers—an artist's fingers—closed around hers, she cursed the voltage that sizzled from their clasped palms up her arm, down her chest and belly to crackle between her legs. If he dipped his eyes, he would catch the hardened tips of her breasts that were probably saluting him from beneath her dress. No more lace bras around this man. Definitely not enough coverage.

Every primal, self-protective instinct within her had her muscles locking in preparation to jerk her hand free. But pride overrode the need, and she met his hazel stare with a steady one of her own. To prove how she refused to let her body's obviously questionable taste rule her, she even squeezed his hand.

But when his nostrils slightly flared and his eyes darkened to an emerald-flecked amber... Oh no, she'd miscalculated. Flames licked at her flesh, and in that instant, she had a vivid premonition of how he would look in the throes of passion. Hooded, but glittering eyes, skin pulled taut over razor-sharp cheekbones, mouth pressed to a flat, almost severe line, and that big, wide-shouldered, powerful frame held rigidly still as he let her adjust to the blazing, overwhelming invasion of him planted deep and firmly inside her.

Pride be damned.

She yanked her hand out of his grip and refused to rub her still-tingling palm against her thigh.

"Why do I think you're lying to me?" he murmured, and after a few seconds of bewilderment, she realized he referred to her weak explanation about her offer of assistance. "What are you hiding, Sophie?"

"I think you're trying to uncover conspiracy theories where there are none," she replied, flippant. "I'm the reporter. That's my job, to be suspicious."

"Where you're concerned, my fail-safe is suspicion." He cocked his head to the side, studying her so closely she sympathized with those butterflies pinned to a corkboard. He wouldn't make her fidget, though. Or make her reveal any of her closely held thoughts regarding him. They were hers, and not his to use to his advantage.

"Then why are you willing to accept my help?" she asked, bristling.

"Maybe for once I'd like to know how it feels to have the press working with me instead of against me. And—" his voice dropped, and an unmistakable growl roughened the tone, causing her flesh to pebble "—I believe in keeping my friends close and my enemies closer. And you, Sophie Armstrong, I plan to be stuck to."

Another threat he would probably call a promise.

A promise that shouldn't have sent waves of molten heat echoing through her.

But it did. They swamped her, and dammit, she wanted to be taken under.

"Like stink on shit, you mean?" she shot back, pouring a bravado she was far from feeling into her tone.

He shifted forward until only scant inches separated them. Like in the gym, his body filled her vision and his warmth reached out for her, surrounding her along with his sandalwood and rain-dampened earth scent. She held her ground, not in the least intimidated as he invaded her personal space. No, not intimidated. She was throbbing. Hungry.

"Closer," he whispered, his breath feathering over her lips in a heavy but light-as-air caress.

Just in time, she caught herself before she tilted her head back, chasing that ephemeral touch.

Okay, screw pride and standing her ground.

Any wise general recognized the wisdom of retreating to fight another day.

And as she pivoted and escaped Joshua's office, she convinced herself she was being wise not running scared.

She almost accomplished the task.

Almost, but not quite.

Five

Joshua pulled open the door to The Java Hut, Falling Brook's upscale coffeehouse on Main Street. The air from the air conditioner greeted him like a lover, wrapping around him with chilled arms of welcome. It might be only May, but the temperature already crept toward the midseventies. And he silently bemoaned the loss of the cooler spring weather. While many people worshipped summer because of days spent on the beaches, lounging by the pool and less clothing, he loved the dynamic and vivid colors and crisp breezes of fall and the rain-scented air and reawakening of life that spring brought.

But no matter which season reigned, coffee remained a constant. And a must.

The fresh, dark aroma of brewing coffee filled the

shop, and he inhaled it with unadulterated pleasure. At nine o'clock on a Saturday morning, he needed caffeine like an addict itching for his next hit. It was his one vice. And yes, he got how pathetic and boring that made him. But considering his father's roaming eye, Jake's wanderlust and Oliver's taste for drugs, he couldn't afford to indulge any. The Lowell men had a proclivity toward addiction, and compared with his father's and brothers', coffee was the least harmful and the only one Joshua could afford.

He glanced down at his watch: 9:11 a.m. Another forty-nine minutes before his mother's doctor's appointment ended, and he had to return to the office and pick her up. Tension tightened his shoulders, and an ache bloomed between them. Deliberately, he inhaled, held the breath and, after ten seconds, released it. The monthly…dammit, not chore. Eve Evans-Janson could never be a chore. Responsibility. As the oldest son, she was his responsibility. But the monthly task of escorting his mother to her doctor always weighed him down like an albatross slung around his neck. Not because he didn't want to be bothered. Never that. He loved Eve, and she'd suffered just as much—if not more—than him and his brothers.

But each visit reminded him of how far she'd deteriorated from the vibrant socialite who'd raised him, loved him and had been his biggest supporter and fan when it'd come to his art. While Vernon hadn't understood and viewed his passion as a passing fancy, his mother had been so proud and celebrated along with him when he'd scored his own gallery show. She'd been his loudest cheerleader.

That woman had disappeared, fifteen years ago, replaced by a quiet, withdrawn recluse who only rarely ventured past the gates of the family's Georgian-style mansion. Her numerous friends had been abandoned and now the butler, maid and chef were her friends. She left the house only for doctor's appointments, the rare appearance at a charity function or the occasions he practically forced her out of the house to go to lunch or dinner with him. Vernon's betrayal had humiliated her. Especially since she'd initially defended him with unshakable faith. When he'd disappeared, she'd believed he might've been kidnapped—or worse. The victim of foul play. But never would he have cheated his clients and friends or stolen from his family and abandoned them to be the recipients of controversy, scorn and pain. Yet, as the days turned into weeks and then months, and the FBI's evidence piled up, Eve had to face the truth— her husband and their father was a criminal who'd bilked millions from those who'd placed their trust in him, then thrown those who'd loved and depended on him the most to the wolves. She'd never recovered.

And now…now he did what he could to ensure she didn't fade away behind the walls that were less her sanctuary and more her prison.

He clenched his fingers into a fist, then purposely relaxed them, exhaling as he did. Dammit, if he had his father here right now, each finger would be wrapped around his neck. Disgust twisted in his chest. If only what he felt toward his father was as simple as anger.

Stepping to the counter, he shoved everything from his mind and focused on ordering. Moments later, with his Americano in hand, he turned toward the entrance, but slammed to a halt.

A petite woman stood next to a table near the huge window, her back toward him, the ends of her unbound hair grazing the tank top—bared skin below her shoulders. The black top molded to the slim line of her back. Dark blue jeans clung to the gentle flare of her hips, the gorgeous tight ass that could be an eighth wonder of the world and legs that could grace a runway and climb the rocky, tough face of a mountain.

An achingly familiar itch tingled in his palms and hands. Familiar and painful. The need to hold a paintbrush. To capture the beauty and strength before him. To immortalize it. His medium had been mixed-media collages, but he'd also loved to paint. And right now he would use bold, rich colors to portray the golden tones of her skin, the power in that tiny body, the larger-than-life vibrancy of her personality, the thick softness of her hair.

That hair.

The thick golden-brown strands reminded him of a mare his father had doted on when Joshua had been a boy. Like raw umber with lighter strands of deep, burnished sunlight. His father had babied that horse, brushing her coat himself until it shined.

A yearning for a return to those idyllic times yawned so wide and deep, Joshua barely managed

to restrain his free hand at his side so he wouldn't
rub the knot that had formed just below his rib cage.

He could hate her alone for dragging that memory out of the abyss even as he fought against the
need to burrow his hands in the wavy mass up to his
wrists, fist it, tug on it... Bury his face in it. He already had personal knowledge of how far he would
have to bend to inhale her citrus-and-flowers scent.
As small as she was, he could completely surround
her. Until he met Sophie Armstrong, tall, statuesque
women had been his type. But now...now he got the
lure of a petite woman he could cover with his big-
ger body. She triggered a primal, almost animalistic
desire in him to take down and conquer her even as
he did everything in his power to drown her in pleasure. Not that Sophie would take anything easily. No,
he imagined she gave as good as she got in bed as
much as she did out...

Molten heat swarmed through him at the thought
of holding those slender, strong arms above her head,
pressing his chest to her small, firm breasts, having
those toned thighs clasping his waist as he drove inside her. She would be so tight, so perfect, damn near
strangling his dick.

As if sensing his scrutiny, Sophie glanced over her
shoulder and met his gaze. Surprise flickered over
her face, her gray eyes widening slightly. He wanted
them to do that when he first pushed into her sex.
Hungered to see them darken like they did now as
she slid a long glance down his body, and he swore
he could feel that perusal as if her fingertips brushed

over his collarbone, chest, abs, thighs…cock. Blood rushed to his flesh, thickening it behind the zipper of his pants. Hell yes, he wanted that touch on his bare skin, light then hard. Gentle then bruising. Yeah, he wanted this fairy of a woman to mark him.

A frigid blast of ice skated over his skin, digging farther to muscle and bone so he was chilled from the inside out.

Of all the women he could get hard over, Sophie Armstrong, reporter for the *Falling Brook Chronicle*, was the absolute last. Just this morning hadn't he witnessed the evidence of her recent rehashing of the scandal with his father in the creases on his mother's face and in the slump of her stooped shoulders? Haley might have managed to nab the paper before it was delivered to his mother's home, but Eve had overheard the maid and butler talking about it in hushed tones. And she'd demanded to see the paper. Reading that article had taken a toll on her.

So even with Sophie's offer to help him determine if the paternity accusation was true or not, he could never trust her. Could never believe that he wasn't just the means to another juicy story. Who knew what her follow-up article would contain? Why the fuck did he agree to it?

No. Sophie was a threat to his business, his family… to his sanity.

But he'd never been led around by his dick, and he wouldn't start a new trend now.

Still, as her lush mouth curled into a smile, he had to remind his body of that.

He tossed his still-full cup in the trash and crossed the room toward her, because no way in hell would he run from her. Or the need that strung his body so tight. It was a wonder he didn't snap in two at the slightest movement.

"Sophie," he greeted, for the first time thankful for the avaricious media and eyes that forced him to perfect a mask of indifference. He swept a glance over the laptop bag that hung near her hip. "Working?"

"Yes, but from home today. I'm a creature of habit, though. Every morning I stop in here for a coffee and their cinnamon-and-brown-sugar scones. Have you had them yet? They're God's way of saying He loves us."

She released a throaty hum that had his gut clenching. Hard. He wanted to hear it again even as he longed to trap the sound inside her...with his mouth.

Goddammit, he needed to get control. And quick.

"No, I can't say I've had the pleasure," he replied. "I'll take your word for it."

She arched a brow. "Oh, really? That would be a first between us."

"Sheathe your sword, Sophie," he said.

"So you finally admit that you need every bit of help you can muster when going up against me?" she challenged, amusement lighting her eyes like glittering stars.

"I never said I didn't. Only a fool would encounter you and not be battle ready with everything in his arsenal available to him."

She heaved an exaggerated sigh and splayed her

fingers wide over her chest. "I do believe that's the nicest thing you've ever said to me."

His wry chuckle caught him by surprise. The last thing he'd ever expected to do with Sophie was laugh. A warning for caution blared in his ears. He couldn't afford to let down his guard, become too comfortable around her.

"What are you doing on this side of town? The coffee here is great, but I've had what you keep at your office and it's pretty good, too."

"I'm not headed to work this morning. I'm waiting for my mother. She has a doctor's appointment right down the street."

She frowned and laid a hand on his lower arm. "I'm sorry. Is she okay?"

For a moment the flare of heat emanating from her touch seared his voice, rendering it useless. She might as well have settled her palm over his dick the way he throbbed and ached.

Gritting his teeth, he ignored the lust coursing through him like a swollen river and said, "Yes. It's just a regular checkup."

"Oh, okay." Her frown deepened for a moment, and it seemed as if she was going to probe further, but in the next instant she skated a quick survey up and down his frame. "So you're not going to the office, but *this* is what you wear on a Saturday morning?"

He didn't bother glancing down to take in the white long-sleeved shirt and black slacks. "Problem?"

She snorted, a smirk flirting with the corners of her lips. "Oh no. No problem at all. I'm just wondering what you wear to bed. An Armani suit? Or maybe a tuxedo."

The humor fled from him, chased away by the desire flaring inside him by the mention of "bed." Hell, she'd reduced him to a fourteen-year-old boy who got hard with the switch of the wind. That didn't stop him from cocking his head to the side and murmuring, "You're wondering what I wear to bed, Sophie? All you have to do is ask."

Slashes of red tinted her cheekbones and her eyes turned to liquid silver. Neither of them spoke as the air hummed with tension, pulsed with an unacknowledged lust volleyed between them. God, he wanted her. Why her—a reporter who sought to paint him as a puppet for his deadbeat father? Would she screw him, then riffle through his drawers to find dirt she could use for the follow-up piece on him and his family?

Something deep inside him objected to that, argued that she wasn't that kind of woman, but this time logic ruled. He'd known too many people who would sooner use him than blink. As a Lowell, men and women looked at him and saw money, connections, information and sometimes a good fuck. But never the man. Never the son struggling to make good and be honorable where his father had failed.

Sophie blinked, the desire clearing from her gaze, and at the same time he edged back a step.

"Pass," she rasped, then, clearing her throat, turned back to her table and gathered up her empty coffee cup, paper plate and plastic fork. "Seriously, though,

Joshua," she continued in a stronger voice, that hint of humor returning. "Jeans. Ever heard of them?"

"Sounds familiar," he drawled, following her toward the exit. She dropped her trash in the receptacle and pushed through the coffeehouse door. "What is this sudden fascination with my clothes?"

She laughed as they moved out onto the sidewalk, stepping aside as more customers entered the café. He ignored the curious glances shot their way. After fifteen years, he should be immune to them. But he'd never managed it. They still got under his skin.

"Not your clothes. I'm just curious if you ever relax. If you're ever not Joshua Lowell of the Falling Brook Lowells, CEO of Black Crescent Hedge Fund and just Josh. Does anyone call you that?"

"My brothers did. But it's been a long time," he murmured.

Just Josh.

There was no such person. Once upon a time there'd been. Josh had been an artist on the precipice of a promising career. He'd been the older brother to Jake and Oliver, who'd been friends as well as brothers. Back before they'd looked on him with scorn and resentment for following in their father's tainted footsteps. Josh had been carefree, laughed often and pursued his passion.

His family and the company wouldn't survive if he reverted to Just Josh.

If he tasted the joy, the life-giving fire of art again, *he* might not survive.

So no, Joshua Lowell, savior and CEO of Black Crescent, was much safer.

Sophie studied him with narrowed eyes, then, slipping the strap of her laptop bag over her head so it crossed her torso, she grabbed his hand in hers and tugged him forward. The shock of her skin touching his reverberated through his body and stunned him long enough that he didn't resist her leading him down the sidewalk. He should pull away from her, cauterize the connection that bled fire into his veins...

He flipped their hands so he enfolded hers, so soft and delicate, in his.

Minutes later, she paused in front of Henrietta's Creamery, the town's only ice-cream shop. He stared at her, confused and more than a little taken aback.

"Ice cream?" he asked, not bothering to eliminate the skepticism from his voice. "At nine thirty in the morning?"

She shook her head and mockingly patted his arm with the hand he wasn't clasping. "See? This right here is what I mean. When is there ever an inappropriate time for ice cream? Joshua, that stick in your ass. Was it surgically implanted, or did it just grow there naturally?"

The bark of laughter abraded his throat, shocking him as much as her teasing. No one would ever dare to say that to him. Hell, no one would dare to tease him. But this slip of a woman knew no boundaries or fear. From the first, she hadn't been cowed or intimidated by him. And God, it felt good.

"Naturally. And it required effort and a lot of pruning and nurturing," he deadpanned, causing a grin to spread wide over her face. Jesus, she was gorgeous.

"Well, I volunteer as tribute to help you remove it. Starting with an ice-cream cone for breakfast. C'mon." She didn't brook any disagreement but jerked on the door to the shop and entered, pulling him behind her.

After a brief but spirited debate over the best flavors, they walked out with two waffle cones topped with a double scoop of ice cream—salted caramel for him and butter pecan for her.

Him.

Joshua Lowell.

Walking down the sidewalk lining Main Street. Eating an ice-cream cone.

Jesus, how did he get here?

But as Sophie tipped her head back and smiled at him, the light of it reflecting in her beautiful gray eyes, he embraced the moment. Embraced, hell. Hoarded it. In less than half an hour, he would be returning to pick up his mother, and the mantle of responsibility that he'd prematurely donned would fall back around his shoulders. Weighing them down with a pressure that was at times suffocating. Pressing them down with an anger-rimmed sadness that he'd never been able to completely banish no matter how many times he'd told himself that they didn't need his father. That they were better off without him.

Yeah, he was going to embrace this moment and grab on to it selfishly. Because as Joshua Lowell, Vernon's son, he didn't have many. The cost for that

kind of greed was too high. As his father's actions
had taught him.

"Now, I don't want to say I told you so…" she said,
an impish smile curving her lips. "Oh hell, who am I
kidding? I *so* do want to say it. I told you so."

"I think you might have held that in for two minutes and twenty-eight seconds," he drawled. "Congratulations."

She twirled her hand in front of her, dipping
slightly at the waist. "Thank you. I'll have you know
my restraint was hard fought."

He snorted, swiping his tongue through the cold
cream and barely managing to contain a moan. When
was the last time he'd indulged like this? Years. It'd
been years.

"I don't want to alarm you, but people are staring," Sophie informed him in a stage whisper. As if
he hadn't already noticed. "One woman just almost
rear-ended the car in front of her at the stoplight." She
gave a mocking gasp, splaying the fingers not holding
the ice-cream cone wide across her chest. "Whatever
do you think it could be that they find so interesting?"

Joshua didn't answer, but some of the peace and
joy filtered from his chest, replaced by a slick, grimy
stain that was a murky mixture of guilt, anger and
helplessness. The sludge tracked its way across his
chest, down to his gut, where it churned. He deliberately relaxed his grip on the cone but couldn't prevent the clenching of his jaw. A hint of neon-red pain
flared along the edge.

"It must be so tiring," Sophie murmured, all notes

of teasing evaporated from her tone. He glanced down at her, and those gray eyes looked back at him, warm and velvet with a sympathy he never believed he'd glimpse. At least not for him.

"What must be tiring?" he ground out.

"Feeling like an animal in a zoo. Always being on display," she replied softly.

Her observation struck too deep...too on point. He hated it that she saw it. Hated more that he'd allowed her to.

"Being fodder for any newspaper or online gossip column," he lashed out with a biting coldness that was meant to burn.

She bent her head over her treat and licked a melting trail of ice cream. In spite of the anger knotting his gut, lust slid through him in a thick glide, flowing straight for his already pulsing flesh. He wanted that delicate pink tongue on him. Trailing over him like he was the most delicious thing she'd ever tasted. He hungered to hear her moans of pleasure in his ears, have it vibrate over his skin.

His control was soaked tissue paper when it came to this woman.

"I left the door wide-open on that one," she said long moments later, voice quiet. "I won't apologize for my job—it's an important one, and I love it. But I will say I'm sorry that it's contributed to making you feel as if you were a fish in a bowl. I can't imagine that kind of scrutiny is easy."

"But deserved, some would say." They continued to walk down the sidewalk in a silence taut with tension.

Or more specifically, the roil of emotions tumbling inside him. Shoving against his sternum, his throat, seeking an escape. A release. "There are days I believe I deserve it. Give people their due. They need to watch me and make sure I'm not exhibiting signs of becoming Vernon Lowell. They have the right to that transparency. Even years later. Even though—"

Even though there were times he wanted to yell that he wasn't his father. That it wasn't him that had wronged them. It wasn't his fault.

But he couldn't. Because in the end, the sins of the father were visited upon the sons.

In their eyes, as the head of Black Crescent, as the only one available to direct their anger and mistrust at, it was his fault.

And he couldn't argue with them. Because deep inside, in that place that creaked open only in the darkest part of night when he had no energy left to keep it closed, he agreed with them.

Beside him, Sophie sighed and tunneled her fingers through her hair, dragging the strands away from her face and offering him an even more unencumbered view of her clean, elegant profile. A small frown wrinkled the smooth skin between her eyebrows.

"Deserve?" she mused almost to herself. She shook her head. "I don't agree with that. While I do believe in the truth and that people have the right to be aware of events that affect their welfare and lives, they aren't owed pieces of a person's security, peace or soul. Each of us should have the right to privacy, and we don't need anyone's permission to covet it or request it. And this is from a reporter." She lightly snorted, again shaking her head. Pausing, she took another swipe of the ice cream, and her tone became more thoughtful than irritated. "My parents divorced when I was almost thirteen, and it was… Well, *unpleasant* would be an understatement. The nasty arguing and name-calling had been bad enough. But they saw me as an ally to be wooed, a prize to be won in a contest. And they attempted this by competing in who could tell me the foulest, most humiliating things about the other. How my father cheated or how my mother had sent them to the poorhouse with her spending. So many things a child shouldn't be privy to, especially about her parents.

"But they twisted the truth about each other in this acrimonious and desperate need to make the other appear as horrible as possible. Never realizing how they were slowly picking me apart ugly word by ugly word. Because all I heard was how it was my fault they were divorcing. My father cheated. That just meant he was so unhappy at home with me for not doing better in school or being a pest at home that he went somewhere else to find happiness. Or if my mother spent too much money, it was on me because I asked for too much."

She inhaled a breath, and he caught the slight tightening of her hold on the cone. After several seconds, she released a trembling but self-deprecating chuckle.

"Sophie…"

But she interrupted him with a wave of her hand.

"No, I know none of that is true. Now, anyway. But back then…" Her voice trailed off, but seconds later, she lifted a slim shoulder in a half shrug. "They made my teenage years hell, but I should thank them. Because of all that, plus the shuffling back and forth to different homes, never feeling truly rooted or secure, I made sure that I would be able to stand on my own two feet as an adult. That no one would ever have the power or ability to ever rip the rug out from under me again. They also directed me on the path to my career. They fueled my desire to filter facts from half-truths or fiction. And, when it was called for, to shield the innocent from it."

He digested that in silence. "Which is why you didn't print the rumors about me having a daughter in the article," he added.

She nodded, not looking at him. "Yes. I know what you think of me, Joshua, but I wouldn't deliberately smear someone's name or hurt them. Not without all the facts that can be backed up and confirmed beyond doubt. Am I perfect? No. But I try to be."

He licked the melting ice cream in his hand, warring within himself about how much he could share with Sophie. Why he *shouldn't* share. But after her baring some of her chaotic childhood, he owed her. Still…

"Off the record?" he murmured.

She jerked her gaze to him, and in the dove-gray depths he easily caught the surprise. And the flicker of irritation. As if annoyed that he'd ask. But as lovely as she was, as honest as she'd been with him, he couldn't forget who she was. *What* she was.

"Of course," she said, none of the contrasting emotions in her eyes reflected in her voice.

"Of course," he repeated softly, staring down at her. *What the hell are you doing?* he silently questioned his sanity, but then said, "I deserve their censure because of my life before my father decided to screw us all six ways to Sunday. Mine was charmed. I won't say perfect, because in hindsight, it wasn't. Nothing is. But for me, it was close. My brothers and I—we didn't have to want for anything. Not material, financial or emotional. Dad was always busy building Black Crescent into one of the foremost hedge funds, but Mom? She'd been there, attentive, supportive, loving. We weren't raised by an army of servants, even though we did have them. But Mom—and even Dad to an extent—had been involved. We attended one of the most exclusive and premier prep schools in the country and, later, Ivy League universities. I knew who I was and what I wanted to be. I never had doubts back then. I held the world in my palm and harbored no insecurities or fears that I could have it all."

"I always wondered about that," Sophie said, that intuitive and insightful gaze roaming his face. "If you faced any backlash or disapproval from your father for choosing art over the family business."

Why the hell am I talking about this? He never discussed his art or his career ambitions. A pit gaped in his chest, stretching and threatening to swallow him whole with the grief, disillusionment and sense of failure that poured out. Those dreams were dead and buried with a headstone to mark the grave.

Forcing the memories and the words past his tightening throat, he barely paused next to a garbage can and pitched his cone into it. He couldn't talk about this and even consider eating. Not with his gut forming a rebellion at just the unlocking of the past.

"From my mother, no. Like I said, she supported me from the very first. When I was a child, she enrolled me in art classes, encouraged me to continue even when my father scoffed at it or dismissed my interest as a passing fancy. But art was...my passion. My true friend, in ways. Growing up in Falling Brook, we had to be careful about image, about never forgetting we were Vernon Lowell's sons and Eve Evans-Janson's sons. There was a trade-off for the life of privilege we led, and that was perfection. But with art? I never had to be perfect. Or careful. I just had to be me. I didn't have to curtail my opinions to make sure I didn't offend anyone or reflect on my father. I could be unfailingly and unapologetically honest. I could trust it more than anything or anyone else."

A vise squeezed his chest so hard, so tight, his ribs screamed for relief. Just talking about that part of him he'd willingly—but without choice—amputated brought ghostly echoes of the joy, the freedom he'd once experienced every time he took a picture, picked up a piece of metal, lifted a paintbrush...

He shook them off, shoving them in the vault of his past and locking the door. If he were going to discuss that part of him, of his life, he had to separate himself from the emotion behind it. Besides, that was who he'd been. That man had ceased to exist the moment his father had gone on the lam, leaving his family and ten others broke and broken.

"But to answer your question, there wasn't any strife. More so because I believe Dad thought I would indulge in art, get it out of my system and then come work for Black Crescent. Even when I scored my first gallery show the summer after I graduated from college, Dad was pleased for me, but he also told me I had a choice to make and he hoped I chose wisely. 'Wisely' being coming into the business with him."

Had his father known even then that he would be going on the run? Had he already planned his escape plan? Because only two months after that conversation, he'd disappeared.

"While researching the article, I always thought that was amazing. Do you know how many artists are capable of getting their own gallery shows so soon in their careers? But then again, I saw pictures of your work. God, you were phenomenal," she breathed.

The unadulterated awe in her voice snagged on something inside him, jerking and tugging as if trying to bring that ephemeral and elusive "thing" to the surface to be acknowledged and analyzed. He shrank from it. Not in the least bit ready to do that.

He never would be.

"Can I ask you something? And disclaimer—it's going to be intrusive," she said, dumping her cone into a nearby trash can before slipping a sidelong glance at him. When he dipped his chin in agreement, she murmured, "How could you step away from it? I'm just thinking of how I would feel if I suddenly lost my career. Or if I couldn't do it anymore. And not just reporting, but my purpose. Empty. And lost. How could you give it up so easily?"

"Easily?" His harsh burst of laughter scraped his throat raw. "There was nothing easy about it, Sophie. I had a choice to make. Family or a career in art." Leave, move to New York to escape the judgment and condemnation and pursue his passion, or stay and save his family and the business. Try to repair what his father had torn apart. Even when Jake had done just that, Josh had stayed. And there'd been nothing simple or easy about that decision. "In the end my father had been right. I would have to choose, and I did. Not that it'd been much of one. I couldn't abandon my family."

Not like him remained unspoken but deafening in the silence that followed his words.

"I'm sorry," she whispered.

He slipped his tightly curled fists into the pockets of his slacks. "For what?" he rasped.

"For assuming it'd been an easy decision. That you had to make it in the first place."

He drew to an abrupt halt, absently thankful they'd made it to the parking lot at the far end of Main where his car waited. Thankful no one loitered in the area, and that for once, they were away from prying eyes.

No one—no *fucking* one—had ever said that to him. Had ever thought to consider the cost of his sacrifice, the effect of it on him. And no one had ever thanked him or sympathized that he'd given up the best part of him to take care of family. A family in which two of its members resented him for making that choice.

Alone. Here, in this parking lot, partially insulated from the public that had judged him so harshly, the remnants of the past clinging to him like skeletal fingers, he could admit that for fifteen years, he'd been so damn alone.

That choice had cost him the closeness he'd once shared with his brothers. It'd stolen the plugged-in mother from his youth. The so-called friends he'd believed he had. Most of all, it'd left him bereft of his dreams and—how had she described it?—empty.

Yes. Empty.

But in this space, in this fleeting moment, he didn't. With this woman, with her silken skin, molten eyes and temptress mouth, he felt…seen. And it sent heat rushing through him like air caught in a wind tunnel—loud, powerful and threatening to rip him apart. He edged his feet apart, slightly widening his stance as if bracing himself against the overwhelming longing to touch, to hold, to *connect*.

He lifted his hand to brush his fingertips over her delicate jaw, waiting, no, expecting, her to wrench away from him to avoid his caress.

She didn't. Sophie stood still, her headed tilted back, gaze centered on him. She didn't flinch from him. Didn't question what the hell he was doing.

No, those sweet lips parted on a soft gasp that went straight to his dick, grazing it.

Locking down a groan behind clenched teeth, he shifted closer, turning slightly to shield her from any curious spectators. A thick cocoon of desire might be enfolding them, but it didn't erase the fact that they stood off Main Street. But where minutes ago that would've prevented him from lowering his head over hers, moving nearer still until his chest pressed against hers and his thighs cradled the slim length of hers, more than ever, he was aware of the disparity in their heights and frames. His body nearly covered her, and the top of her head just barely skimmed his chin. The surge of lust sweeping through his veins, lighting them like an SOS flare, competed with the urge to protect. The impulse to conquer warred with the need to shelter. But instead of being torn in two by the opposing instincts, they melded, mating. Assuring him he could do both. That, by God, he *should* do both.

His fingers continued to explore her jaw, her cheek, the thinner skin over her temple, the slope of her nose in spite of the lust baying in his head like howling dogs. He followed the graceful arches of her eyebrows before traveling back down to trace the upper curve of her mouth, linger in the shallow dip in the middle. Then, he moved to that plumper bottom lip, savoring the soft give of it under his fingertips. He didn't offer just his thumb the treat of it. All his fingertips got in on the pleasure of the caress.

Her breath hitched, and again he fought back a moan at the gentle gust of air against his suddenly overly sensitive skin. Words crowded at the back of his throat.

Tell me I can have this temptation of a mouth that has woken me up, hard and hurting, for days now.

Will you let me fuck this mouth, Sophie? Will you let me defile it so you can taste the dirtiness of my kiss for days? Weeks?

But he didn't utter them. Instinct warned him that breaking this lust-drenched and pulsing silence with any sound would rip this opportunity away from him. Shatter the cords that held them here in this moment—cords that shimmered with heat but were as fragile as glass.

He'd hungered for this chance for too long. Battled himself over it too hard to abdicate it.

So, instead, he planted his thumb in the middle of the bottom curve, pressed until the tip of his finger grazed the edges of her teeth. When she didn't draw away from him but tilted her head forward to lean into the pressure, he shuddered.

And when she parted those beautiful lips and flicked her tongue over his flesh, he had his answer.

Not bothering to trap his groan in this time, he dipped his head and took her. Releasing the greedy sound into her mouth, replacing his thumb with the slick glide of his tongue.

God, the taste of her.

Sweet like the butter-pecan ice cream she'd been eating. Sultry like air thick and perfumed after a spring rain. Heady like a shot of whiskey. Deliciously wicked. Like sex.

With hands going rough with greed, he burrowed one into her hair, fisting the strands and tugging. Tugging until her mouth was right where he wanted it... needed it. Her swallowed her small whimper, giving her a growl in return as she opened wider for him. Granting him entrance to her. To heaven.

He thrust between those beautiful lips, tangling his tongue with hers, dancing, dueling. Because Sophie wasn't a passive participant. Just as she challenged him in his office, in a newspaper conference room or a gym, she gave as good as she got here, as well. She sucked and licked, stroking into his mouth to demand and take.

His grip on her hair and hip tightened, dragging her closer, impossibly closer. His hips punched forward, grounding his erection against the softness of her belly. Fire ripped a scorching path up his spine, then back down to his dick. Jesus, she was about to set him off like a teenager copping his first feel behind the gym bleachers. Cocking his head, he delved deeper, a desperate hunger for more digging into him. One nip of her lips, one sample of her taste, and he was hooked, ravenous for more.

"Josh," she breathed against his damp lips. Hearing the abbreviated version of his name had his flesh hardening further, had him aching. And he couldn't not reward her—hell, thank her—with another drugging kiss and roll of his hips.

The ring of a phone shattered the thick haze of lust that enclosed them.

He lifted his head, the air in his lungs ragged and

harsh. She stared up at him, those storm-gray eyes clouded with the same desire coursing through him like electrified currents. Her swollen mouth, wet from his tongue, glistened, and he'd lowered his head, submitting to the sensual beckoning of them when the peal of the phone jangled again.

Dammit.

Disentangling his hands from her hair and releasing the sweet curve of her hip, he stepped back, reaching in his pocket for his silent cell phone. At the same time, Sophie retrieved hers from the front pocket of her bag. Tapping the screen, she held the cell to her ear.

"Hi, Althea," she said, her gaze meeting his for a second before she turned away. Althea Granger, the editor in chief of the *Falling Brook Chronicle*. Her boss. "Yes, that's not a problem. Has anyone else picked up the story yet?"

A frigid deluge of water crashed over him in a wave.

For moments, he'd felt young again. Free again. He'd allowed himself to forget who Sophie was. Who he was. But reality had a way of slapping the hell out of a person and reminding him that life wasn't handholding and ice-cream cones or kissing a beautiful woman. It was hard, sometimes grueling work, disappointment and constantly brushing off scraped knees and bruised hands to get up and face it again.

He could still taste the unique and addictive flavor of her on his lips, his tongue. But he couldn't let Sophie Armstrong in. And her being a reporter was just one reason. A very good reason to keep his distance from her, but not the only one.

When Vernon had left, he'd broken his ability to trust. And his brothers had trampled on the pieces on their way out of Falling Brook. Even his mother had abandoned him. Not physically, but definitely emotionally. When he loved people, when he let them in, they left. They eventually abandoned him.

They eventually devastated him.

No, he couldn't trust Sophie. Leaving himself vulnerable again came at too high a price. And he had nothing left to pay it with.

"Okay, I'll head to the office now. See you in a few." Sophie ended the call and faced him again. "Sorry about that." She cleared her throat, twin flags of pink staining the slants of her cheekbones. Left over from their kiss—if that was what that clash of mouths, tongues and teeth could be labeled—or from the phone call. "I need to go into work for a few hours."

"I heard," he said, deliberately infusing a sheet of ice into his voice. As if just seconds ago it hadn't been razed to hell by lust. He glanced down at his watch. "That's fine. I have to leave, too." While he'd been taking her mouth, time had raced by, and he was due to pick up his mother in five minutes. But the errand was just a handy excuse to put distance between him and Sophie. Because in spite of his resolve and the reminder of why he couldn't become involved with her, he still had to threaten himself with self-harm to avoid staring at her mouth like a marauding beast. "Have a good weekend, Sophie."

Not waiting on her reply, he pivoted on his heel and strode back in the direction they'd come. And if that cloak of loneliness settled across his shoulders again, well, it was preferable to pain.

Preferable to betrayal.

And Sophie smacked of both.

Six

Sophie wove a path among the many businessmen, socialites, philanthropists and even a handful of celebrities crowded into the Ronald O. Perelman Rotunda of the Guggenheim Museum in Manhattan. The annual Tender Shoots Art Gala brought all the tristate area's glitterati out in support of the New York–based arts program.

Taking a sip of her cocktail, she dipped her head in a shallow nod at a woman whose diamond necklace and ruby-red strapless gown could probably pay off the entirety of Sophie's student loans. She held her head up, meeting the assessing gaze of every person she had eye contact with. Or maybe it just felt assessing to her. As if they were attempting to peer beneath the expertly applied makeup and strapless, glittery, floor-length dress that she'd needed a crowbar and a prayer to squeeze into in order to determine if she belonged.

Well, at an invite-only event that required fifteen thousand a plate fee plus a hefty donation for entrance, she didn't belong. She'd grown up in Falling Brook, one of the most exclusive, wealthiest communities along the Eastern Seaboard, but her family had been among the few middle-class residents who either owned businesses in town or worked for Falling Brook Prep, the independent K–twelve school. The kind of excess and luxury represented in the grand, open space surrounded by the spiral-ramped architecture capped by a gorgeous skylight exceeded her imagination and bank account. Thank God, Althea's partner was a stylist who had let Sophie borrow a designer gown for the night. And didn't that just increase the surreal feeling of Cinderella attending the ball before her carriage turned back into a pumkin that had filled her since stepping onto the curb outside the famous museum?

If not for Althea receiving an invitation because of the paper's piece about the event, the organization and the underprivileged youth it benefited, Sophie would be home, catching up on season two of *The Handmaid's Tale*. But since it'd been Sophie's article that had garnered the invite, Althea had convinced her to accept and attend. She should be grateful and flattered. But while she had no problem reporting on the country's wealthy elite, she drew a line at socializing with them. It reminded her too much of a time in her life when she'd been blinded by their world and the man she'd once loved who'd belonged to it.

Too bad she hadn't remembered not to cross that line that morning with Joshua Lowell.

A convoluted mixture of embarrassment, self-directed anger and a relentless, aching need jumbled and twisted deep inside her. Just thinking of how he'd cupped her jaw, gently caressed her face and then claimed her mouth had her shouting obscenity-laced reprimands at herself…even as she pressed her thighs together to fruitlessly attempt to stifle the throbbing ache in her sex. And all that led to her embarrassment. The man had sexed her mouth, then walked away from her without a backward glance. As if that devastation of a kiss hadn't affected him at all. If not for the insistent, commanding grind of his thick erection against her belly, she would've believed he hadn't been.

But no matter that he'd moaned into her mouth and had granted her a clear premonition of what it would be like to be controlled and branded by that big, wide-shouldered body, he *had* transformed from the approachable, almost vulnerable man who'd strolled down Main Street with her, licking ice cream in a way that had her sex ready to throw itself at his feet, to an iceberg who'd dismissed her as if their connection had been of no consequence. As if *she* were of no consequence. And hell, maybe to him, she wasn't.

Staring down into the glass, she didn't see the pale gold champagne but his shuttered expression and flat stare as she'd ended her phone call. A shiver ran through her, as if the ice that had entered that measured inspection skated over her exposed skin now. She didn't believe in deluding herself; she acknowledged that it'd been Althea's call that had changed him. He'd no doubt suddenly been reminded of what they were to one another. She was the woman who had dragged the darkest, most scandalous parts of his history back out, dusted them off and planted them on the front page of the newspaper for public consumption. Again.

Half of her was surprised he hadn't asked her if that kiss was off the record. Despite her best efforts, her lips twisted into a slight sneer. As if she'd treat him to an ice-cream cone just to butter him up for a scoop—no pun intended. Screw it. That pun was totally intended.

Smothering a sigh, she lifted her fluted glass to her lips and sipped. At least this gala provided one purpose. Distract her from thoughts of—

Joshua.

Her gaze locked with a beautiful and all too familiar pair of hazel eyes. Lust gut-punched her like a prizefighter with a penchant for ear biting. If not for her locked knees and sheer grit not to humiliate herself in the four-inch stilettos, the blow would've knocked her on her ass. Beneath the bandage-style bodice of her dress, her nipples drew into taut, pebbled points begging for just a whisper of a caress from those long, blunt-tipped fingers. Pinpricks of electricity rippled up and down her exposed spine, sizzling in the base of her spine. And her feminine flesh… She stifled a needy and shameful moan. Her flesh swelled, damp and sensitive from just a hooded glance from those green-and-gold and way too perceptive eyes.

Good God, had she conjured him with her own wayward thoughts?

"Ms. Armstrong?" a low, cultured voice called her name, and Sophie yanked her scrutiny away from Joshua. A tall, powerfully built and handsome man stood next to her. Black hair waved back from a high forehead, emphasizing a face with strong facial features, a full, sensual mouth and intense blue eyes. He smiled, flashing perfect white teeth. "You are Sophie Armstrong, correct?" he asked, extending a large hand toward her.

"Yes," she replied, accepting the hand. He squeezed it lightly before releasing it. "I'm sorry, do we know one another?"

"No, we haven't officially met. But I've followed your career these past few years from Chicago to the *Falling Brook Chronicle*. I'm a fan of your journalistic style. Most recently, I enjoyed the pieces you wrote on the Tender Shoots Arts Council as well as the one on the Black Crescent scandal. Considering the topic and the many times it's been reported on, I thought you wrote an objective, well-researched article. Especially about Joshua Lowell and his former art career. I don't think many people remember the accomplished artist he was and the potential career he once had."

Accomplished artist he is.

The words burned on her tongue. No one with the kind of talent she'd seen in his work or whose voice contained the passion his had while describing what art had meant to him could turn off the God-given gift he'd been blessed with. Joshua might be the CEO of his father's company, but now more than ever after this morning's conversation with him, she was convinced the artist who'd created such awe-inspiring, magnificent pieces of art still existed beneath those expensive, perfectly tailored suits.

"Thank you. I appreciate the compliment, Mr...." She trailed off. The man still hadn't given her his name.

A half smile quirked one corner of his mouth. "Christopher Harrison. I'm one of the organizers of the gala and on the board of trustees for the Tender Shoots Arts Council."

"Mr. Harrison." She nodded. "It's a pleasure to meet you."

"Christopher, please. The pleasure is mine." He crooked an arm and held it out to her. "Can I escort you into dinner? I believe we're sitting at the same table."

A little bemused, she settled her hand in the bend of his elbow. "I'm sitting at your table?" she repeated, unable to keep out the edge of incredulity.

He chuckled. "I confess to using my position with the organization to finagle a favor and moving your seat." He shrugged, but nothing about him said *repentant*. "It's one of the perks of the job."

"Do I need to be worried about why you want my company at your table?" she mused, part of her amused, but the other part wary. Years ago, another sophisticated, handsome man had approached her at a function. And his motives had been anything but pure. Too bad that by the time she'd figured that out, he'd nearly devastated her heart and her integrity. Old suspicions died hard.

Speaking of suspicions…

The charged tingle dancing across the nape of her neck informed her where Joshua stood. And she directed her glance in that direction. Immediately, his hazel gaze snared hers. Burning into hers. For a second, it released her to flicker to the man guiding her through the throng of people. Even across the distance, she caught the firming of his full lips, the darkening of his eyes. And when he returned his narrowed scrutiny to her, the fire in them seared over her exposed skin.

She sucked in a breath, jerking her head forward. Because she needed to pay attention to where her feet and the man next to her were taking her.

Not because she could no longer stand meeting that slightly ominous stare that had heat spiking in her body like she'd transformed into a thermometer.

At least that was what she told herself. As she settled at one of the tables closest to the dais erected at the far end of the rotunda, she continued to remind herself of that. And even as the electrified crackle hummed under her skin, she refused to allow her attention to slip toward the table to her right. Joshua Lowell was just a man. Yes, a beautiful, imposing man who wore a tuxedo as if it'd been created with the sole purpose of adorning that tall, powerful body.

A complicated man who was like a puzzle missing several pieces. Pieces she wanted to hunt down and fit into the empty spaces so she could determine who he really was. The arrogant, commanding CEO with the icy reserve? Or the passionate artist who revealed tantalizing glimpses of vulnerability and kissed like he could consume a woman whole and make her beg him to take more?

He's a man who wants revenge because of the story you wrote on him and his family. A man who denies the existence of his child and is using you to control if you reveal it or not.

Or maybe one who just desperately sought to discover if he truly had a daughter that he'd known nothing about?

Jesus, she was arguing with herself. It was official. Joshua—or this unwarranted and dangerous fascination with him—was driving her nuts.

That same fascination had her casting a glance to the neighboring table. She was a masochist. There was no other explanation. And yet, she found herself once more helplessly ensnared by a copper-and-emerald stare as she'd been in the reception area.

Flayed. That was what that intense, gorgeous and entirely too-perceptive scrutiny did to her. Leave her flayed, open and exposed. Did he see the dueling emotions he stirred in her—the desire for distance, to borrow some of that renowned aloofness, and the desire to feel the intimidating thick length of him again. Not against her stomach this time, but inside her. Stretching her. Marking her.

The woman next to Joshua, a stunning redhead in a black sequined dress that screamed couture, leaned into him, whispering in his ear. He turned to her, releasing Sophie from their visual showdown.

A shaft of…something hot and ugly pierced her chest. She couldn't identify it. *Wouldn't* identify it. Because it wasn't jealousy. The woman, with the onyx jewels dripping from her ears and encircling her neck, belonged to his world. They were perfect for each other.

"Do you know Joshua?" Christopher's question yanked her from the rabbit hole that she'd been in the process of tumbling down. She met his curious gaze. Saw when it flickered toward the other table and Joshua and returned to her. "Are you two acquainted?"

"God, no," she denied with a small deprecating chuckle. Not a lie, exactly. She doubted anyone really *knew* Joshua Lowell. And something whispered that he preferred it that way. "I just wrote an article on one of the darkest periods in his and his family's lives. I'm sure he's not a fan of mine."

"Hmm." Christopher studied her, and she refused to fidget beneath that assessing regard. "I can understand that, I guess. Although, like I mentioned earlier, all things considered, it was a fair piece." He lifted a glass of wine and sipped from it, continuing to study her over the rim. "He's one of our major contributors to the nonprofit. Not surprising, really, with his own background in art."

Yes, she could see that. He might not create pieces

anymore but imagining him pouring financial support into the lives of underprivileged youth so they might have the advantages of following the path he'd walked away from wasn't hard.

Still… She glanced over at one of the walls where numerous canvases, pen-and-ink drawings and framed photographs hung. The oversize, mixed-media collages that used to be Joshua's trademark would seamlessly fit in here. Did he ever wish they were? Did he ever dream of walking into this famed museum and seeing his pieces adorning these off-white walls?

Did it cause him pain to attend a gala celebrating art knowing he couldn't have this? Knowing others were doing what he'd been created to do?

She forced herself not to look at Joshua this time. Afraid she would see what she wanted to instead of who he really was. Maya Angelou had said, "When someone shows you who they are, believe them the first time." That day she'd barged into his office, he'd shown her the ruthless, dismissive and cold business-man. She needed to remember that, brand that image into her mind so when she started to visualize more—a sensitive, burdened man who grieved all that he'd lost—she'd shut that down.

And if that didn't work, remember Laurence Dan-vers. Remember how she'd spectacularly crashed and burned by almost choosing a man over her career, over her ethics. She'd paid for those errors in judg-ment, for her willing blindness.

Never again, though.

Returning her attention to Christopher, she finished dinner with a smile and surprisingly entertaining conversation. Charismatic and funny, he effortlessly charmed her, and when the dishes were cleared and the guests headed back toward the reception area for dancing and more cocktails, she accepted his invitation to join him out on the dance floor.

Tilting her head back, she smiled up at him. "Not that I doubt you could enjoy my company, but, call it a reporter's intuition, I just have the sense you didn't seek me out because of my smile. Or this dress. As gorgeous as it may be."

He grinned, his fingers tightening around her fingers. "It is that, but not as beautiful as the woman wearing it." When she arched an eyebrow, he tipped his head back, laughing. And drawing the attention of the couples swaying to the jazz music along with them. "Your reputation for a no-nonsense investigative journalist is well earned, Sophie Armstrong. I did have an ulterior motive when I approached you this evening."

"I'm waiting."

"Our nonprofit is always seeking out new ways to bring in donations and media coverage that will result in even more donations. Funding and philanthropic gifts are this organization's lifeblood," he said, the humor evaporating from his voice and the intensity that had radiated from him since their initial meeting intensified. "I read your article on the Lowell family and Black Crescent. But my particular interest in the piece was the attention placed on Joshua Lowell. The artist submerged, if I remember correctly. It started me thinking. What if the artist reemerged? Returned to the world where he once stood on the cusp of a promising career? Can you imagine the stir and the money that would bring to Tender Shoots?"

Against her will, excitement kindled in her chest. Yes, she could imagine this. All too easily. Maybe not if she hadn't walked along a sidewalk with him and caught the embers of a deliberately banked passion in his eyes, in his words. But Christopher was correct on all accounts. Joshua returning to the art world would be huge—for both the nonprofit and him.

"I agree it would benefit all involved," she replied vaguely. "But what does it have to do with me?"

"I have an admission to make, Sophie," he said, and unlike his playful confession earlier about the seating arrangements, this one caused an unsettling dip in her stomach. "After the article in the *Falling Brook Chronicle*, I researched you. I believe you, more than anyone, can appreciate the need to protect my sources, but despite telling me earlier that you didn't know him, I discovered you were spotted in Joshua Lowell's company several times."

She remained silent, not confirming or denying. But her heart thundered against her rib cage. Though there'd been nothing untoward or illicit about their meetings—*don't even* think *about the kiss!*—just the perception of conflict of interest could be detrimental to her reputation and career. Her original instinct to be wary around Christopher deepened, and she schooled her features into a polite but distant mask.

"I can guess what you're assuming, Sophie, and you're wrong," he murmured, voice gentling. "I don't intend to accuse you of anything or use my information against you or him."

"Then what are your intentions?" she demanded.

"I need your help in convincing him to consider a showing next year. Just because of who he is—the CEO of Black Crescent Hedge Fund—but also because of how he walked away from what critics had predicted to be an important art career."

Before he finished speaking, Sophie was already shaking her head. "I don't know why you'd think I possess the influence to convince Joshua Lowell to do anything, but—"

"Because I've seen how he hasn't been able to tear his gaze off you all evening. And how you've pretended not to notice—when you haven't been staring back at him," he interrupted. "Tell me I'm wrong."

Her pulse was a deafening beat in her ears, in her blood. "You're wrong," she rasped. And hated that her voice held the consistency of fresh-out-the-package sandpaper. "We barely know each other. And even if we were…more acquainted, Joshua Lowell has buried that side of himself. And it would take much more than a few words from me to resurrect it." *But what if there was a chance for him to discover his passion again?* She waved the hand that'd been resting on Christopher's shoulder. To dismiss his request or her own thoughts? Both applied. And anyway, it wasn't her business. Joshua wasn't her business. "I'm sorry, Christopher. I've enjoyed your company tonight, but your efforts on me were wasted. What you're look-ing for is a miracle, and unfortunately, I'm not in that market."

A sardonic smile curved a corner of his mouth, although his gaze on her remained sharp. Too sharp. "Okay, Sophie. But, if you please, just think about what I'm asking. And if one day you do find yourself in the position to carry influence with him, I and my organization would appreciate it if you would broach the possibility of a show with him. It would help so many students and could very well affect lives."

"Really?" she drawled. "The change-lives card? You're pulling out the big guns."

He chuckled, squeezing her fingers. "I'm nothing if not persistent and shameless."

Thankfully, he dropped the subject. But after their dance ended and she strolled off the crowded floor, a weariness crept over her. She was ready to call it an evening and moved across the room, remov-ing her cell from her purse to place a call to the car service that had picked her up and dropped her off here hours ago. Accepting her thin wrap from the coat check minutes later, she stepped out into the warm May evening. Sounds and scents of the City That Never Sleeps echoed around her—honks, voices carried in the night, exhaust from the passing traf-fic and the frenetic energy that popped and crackled in the air. There'd been a time when she'd believed her future lay in New York or a busy city like it. But Falling Brook, with its slower pace and smaller population, was home, and she wouldn't want to live anywhere else.

"Leaving so early?"

She shivered as the deep, dark timbre of the voice that held a hint of gravel rolled over her. Vibrated within her. Tightening the wrap around her shoulders, she glanced at Joshua. Several inches separated them, but the distance meant nothing with that stare blazing down at her. Lighting her up. Pebbling her nipples. Wetting the insides of her thighs. Another tremble worked its way through her, and those narrowed eyes didn't miss her reaction.

"Are you cold?" he asked, already slipping out of his tuxedo jacket. The relief coursing through her that he'd misperceived the source of that shiver stripped her of her voice. But Joshua didn't need her answer. He shifted closer and draped the garment over her shoulders. Immediately, his delicious sandalwood-and-rain scent enveloped her, surrounded her as effectively as if it were his arms warming her instead of his jacket.

"Thank you," she finally said, mentally wincing at the hoarseness of her tone.

He nodded. A valet approached them, and Joshua handed him a slip of paper. After the young man strode away, Joshua returned his regard to her, sliding his hands into his pants pockets. "You're ending the evening before it's over?" he rumbled. "Did Christopher Harrison say or do something to make you uncomfortable enough to leave?"

"No," she said, adding a sharp head shake for emphasis. "He was fine. I'm just…tired. And I have a forty-five-minute ride ahead of me. So I'm getting a head start."

"You're driving?"

"Althea arranged a car service for me."

He didn't reply, but the full, sensual curves of his mouth tightened at the corners. He'd had a similar reaction to her editor in chief's name earlier today. As if he resented the sound of it.

"What are you doing out here?" she asked, glancing over her shoulder in the direction of the museum. "From what I saw, you seemed to be having a good time."

And by "good time" she meant the statuesque, gorgeous redhead he'd been seated next to at dinner. The ear whisperer. When she'd left the reception area for the coat check, Sophie had been unable to not take note of Joshua. And he'd stood on the rim of the dance floor, the other woman plastered to his side closer than ninety-nine was to a hundred. God, she sounded bitchy to her own self.

"Were you watching me, Sophie?" he murmured, that dark-as-sin voice dipping lower, stroking her skin in a smoky caress.

"Were you watching me, Joshua?" she volleyed back, just as quietly.

They stared at one another, the challenge they'd lobbied between them vibrating. The air thickened, taut with the tension emanating from their bodies.

"Come home with me."

The request edged with demand struck her in

the chest. She locked her knees, but that only prevented her from falling onto her ass. It didn't prevent her mentally wheeling and sprawling in shock. She blinked up at him, felt her eyes widening, and her lips parted on a gasp she couldn't contain.

"What?" she breathed.

"Come home with me," he repeated in that slightly impatient tone that hummed with notes of frustration, anger and even surprise. But not directed at her. Through her rapidly ebbing surprise, she suspected all that emotion was aimed at himself. "I'll take you back to Falling Brook, but come home with me first. We need a place where we can talk openly... privately."

"About what?" she questioned, her heart racing for and nestling in her throat.

"About business that is just between us," he replied, purposefully vague, she suspected. Here, in front of the Guggenheim and anyone walking the Manhattan streets, he wouldn't be more specific than that.

She studied him, her grip tight on her sequined clutch. Alone with Joshua. For possibly hours. Her mind—and common sense—balked. Absolutely not. The last time they'd been together, within feet of Main Street, he'd shown her the real purpose of her mouth. To mate with his. What would happen without the chance of prying eyes catching them? Without the constraints of being in public? He would probably be able to maintain his intimidating control, but her? She wouldn't advise any Vegas high rollers place bets on her. This man was proving to be her weakness, the chink in her professional and personal armor, and getting close enough to let him chip away more was lunacy.

Yet… She stared into his eyes. And almost glanced away from the coolness there. But at the last second, she looked deeper. And caught the shadows of need, of…loneliness. Both echoed within her, and something inside her reacted to them. Reached for them. For him.

Instinctively, she stepped back and away from him. To protect herself. But not from him. Herself. It'd been this same longing to soothe, to please, to be loved that had led her down the wrong path before. With Laurence, she'd been blind. But now, her eyes were wide-open to who and what Joshua was. And if she traveled this road, she would have only herself to blame for the catastrophic results to her career, her integrity, her heart. And God, she harbored zero doubts he would decimate her heart, leaving not even ashes behind.

"Come with me, Sophie," he murmured, holding out a hand to her as the valet pulled to the curb in a sleek black sports car that even her limited knowledge identified as an Aston Martin.

She stared at that palm with fascination, yearning and trepidation. Yes, she wanted him—what was the point in lying about the plain, bald-faced truth? But her body didn't rule her. Not anymore. If he intended to discuss her help on the paternity issue, they definitely couldn't do it out here on the sidewalk where anyone could overhear. And, her inner reporter chimed in, if he went off the record with her before, maybe he would agree to going back on and be willing to let her get that interview he'd denied her for the original story. Her deadline for the follow-up article was fast approaching.

And maybe she was just trying to justify her reasons for unwisely accepting his invite.

"Okay," she said quietly, slipping her hand over his and locking down the shiver that wanted to ripple through her as his fingers wrapped around hers. "But just for a couple of hours."

He nodded, his intense perusal scanning her face, then dipping down her body before returning to her eyes. Without a word, he escorted her to his waiting car. Within moments, she was tucked against the sinfully luxurious leather seat with Joshua behind the wheel. When he pulled away from the curb and merged with the moderate traffic, she couldn't help but admire the expert manner in how he handled the vehicle. A begrudging but warm throb settled just under her navel. If the man wielded such control over this four-thousand-pound rocket, how much would he exert in other places? Or... What would he look like if he loosened the reins on it?

Not my business, she informed herself with a mental sneer. Turning her attention to her phone, she called the car service back and canceled her ride. Then she settled back against the seat for the forty-five-minute ride back to Falling Brook. Other than asking her if the air was too cold and if she was comfortable, they barely uttered a word. But it didn't matter. The screaming tension crowded into the car with them did most of the speaking.

By the time he guided the car into the underground parking lot of a tall brick apartment building, she practically vibrated with the strain of fighting the desire coiled so tight within her and pretending as if he didn't affect her. Business. This was about the article. About their side investigation. She could keep it professional, because that was who she was.

Pep talk delivered, she didn't wait for him to round the car and open the door, but pushed it open herself and exited. He wouldn't open doors for his colleagues at Black Crescent, so he shouldn't for her, either.

Coward. You just don't want him any closer than necessary.

She flipped her inner know-it-all the finger.

And if she stiffened but didn't shift away from the broad hand he settled at the small of her back, well... She just didn't want to be rude.

Joshua led her to an elevator, and soon they were alighting from it into a huge apartment that could've fit her whole childhood home inside. She couldn't trap the gasp that escaped from her. Just as the charity event had exposed her to another level of wealth and luxury, so did his place.

Gleaming and pristine floor-to-ceiling windows that offered an unhindered and gorgeous view of Falling Brook and beyond. A king surveying his kingdom. The impression whispered through her head, and she had to agree. Shaking her head, she moved far-

ther into the foyer, taking in the rest of his space. An
open floor plan that allowed each room to flow seamlessly into the next. A sunken living room, freestanding fireplace, dining room with a table large enough
to fit a large family with no trouble, a large kitchen
with a floating island, beautiful oak cabinets and what
appeared to be stainless steel, state-of-the-art appli-
ances. Because why not? Although, something told
her he most likely used the double-door refrigera-
tor for takeout instead of cooking with the wide six-
burner stove and oven.

Beyond her stretched a dim but deep hallway, and
just off the living room stretched a railless staircase
to an upper level. Expensive-looking but comfortable
furniture filled the vast space, but there was something missing.

Art.

No paintings decorating the cream-colored, freestanding walls. No sculptures that people often staged
on tables or in the wide foyer. Not even a knickknack
on an end table. The absence glared at her, and she
glanced sharply at Joshua, who remained standing
next to her, watching her survey his private sanctuary.

"Let me take this for you." He settled his hands
on her shoulders and his jacket that she still wore.
Though it was undoubtedly made of the finest wool,
it should've disintegrated under the heat from his
palms. Grinding her teeth against the inappropriate
response, she nodded. "Would you like a drink?" he
asked, opening a door behind them and hanging up
the jacket and her wrap.

"Sure." She headed toward the living room, where a large and fully stocked bar stood next to the dark fireplace.

"What would you—" His phone rang, cutting him off. He removed it from his pants pocket and glanced at the screen. "I need to take this. Help yourself, and I'll be right back." Pivoting, he headed toward the hallway, pressing the cell to his ear. "Joshua Lowell."

She stared after him for several moments as he disappeared into a room, shutting it quietly behind him. Only then did she move into the living room, releasing a heavy sigh.

A scotch sounded really good right about now.

Before long, she had a finger of the amber alcohol in a squat tumbler, and she raised it to her mouth for a slow, small sip. She hummed in appreciation at the full-bodied, smooth taste as it burned a path over her tongue and down her throat, settling a ball of warmth in her chest.

"Wow, that's good," she muttered, taking and savoring another mouthful.

Grasping the glass between her hands, she headed toward one of the windows and the magnificent and tranquil view. But there was a scattering of papers on the low chrome-and-glass table in front of the couch. How hadn't she noticed it before? The haphazard pile contrasted so sharply with the pristine order of everything else in the room. Hell, the apartment.

Unable to resist the lure it presented, she approached the table. Guilt crept inside her. Joshua hadn't invited her here to snoop. Yet, she still peered down at the papers.

A printout of names and notes written beside each in his heavy scrawl. Women's names. Now, even if God himself came down and admonished her for breaking the eleventh commandment—thou shall not poke thy nose into thy neighbor's business—she still wouldn't have been able not to look.

She recognized some of the names. A high-powered attorney who lived there in Falling Brook. A society darling known for her parties and benevolent efforts. A B-list actress one blockbuster away from catapulting onto the A-list. And about three other names she didn't recognize. But each one had dates typed next to them. Then a handwritten note about whether Joshua had called, made contact and the result.

No baby.

Child but two years old. Not the right age.

Has a little boy. Same age, wrong sex.

Her grip on the glass of scotch tightened until her fingers twinged in protest. Joshua hadn't been idle. This list bore that out. A list that apparently included the names of women he'd been intimate with in the last four years, if the earliest date was an indication. She wrestled down the hot flare of dark and unpleasant emotion that flashed to life in her chest and twisted her belly. Six women wasn't a lot, but damn, she resented each one because they'd experienced the passion he'd very briefly unleashed on her. With grim effort, she refocused on the paper in front of her. Joshua had clearly been working on finding the woman who was supposed to have birthed his child.

Shock and a softer, far more precarious emotion stirred behind her breastbone, melting into her veins like warm butter. Lifting her free hand, she rubbed the heel of her palm over her heart. Since her offer to Joshua on Wednesday to help research more about the DNA report, she'd done some digging. But she kept hitting dead ends.

She wouldn't stop investigating but... Could the DNA results have been mistaken? Either that or Joshua's outrage at her accusation of being an absentee father had been genuine, and he really didn't know he had a child out there. He hadn't left these papers out for her benefit, because he couldn't have predicted they would meet tonight. Briefly closing her eyes, she ran his past reactions in her head like a movie reel. The pain, anger and, yes, grief. Viewed in a different, more objective lens, she had only one conclusion.

She believed him.

"Snooping, Sophie?"

Body jerking in surprise, she tugged her scrutiny from the table to meet Joshua's hooded gaze. So absorbed in what she'd discovered, she hadn't heard him enter the room. But he stood several feet away, head cocked to the side, studying her with an impenetrable expression. Didn't matter, though. The anger emanated from him, sending the guilt in her belly into a tighter, faster tailspin.

"Yes," she admitted quietly. If her honesty startled

him, he didn't reveal it. That shuttered mask didn't alter. "I'm sorry. I shouldn't have invaded your privacy."

He didn't reply, his eyes narrowing further. Finally, he closed the short distance between them. But he didn't approach her but headed to the bar and fixed a drink. Turning to face her moments later with a tumbler in hand, he continued to study her, slowly sipping.

"Go ahead and ask," he said, his tone as dark and smooth as the alcohol in his hand. "Don't hold back. Isn't that—" he waved the glass in the direction of the table and papers "—what you're here for?"

"Yes," she replied. It was the reason. At least the least complicated and safer reason. And the only one she wanted to admit to. "From your notes, I'm assuming you didn't find a woman with a child or if she did have one, not a child who was the correct age or gender."

He shook his head, tipping his drink up for another swallow. "No. None of them are behind the email you received or the DNA report. I'm not any closer to finding out the truth about whether or not I have a daughter."

"Is this list…complete?" She hated to ask—part of her didn't want to know the answer. No. More specifically, didn't want to know if there were more names. Not when a kernel of resentment and envy lodged just under her breastbone. But the question needed to be posed.

Joshua stared at her for several seconds before

tipping his head back and loosing a hard and loud crack of laughter. But no hilarity laced the jagged edges of it.

"You're asking if I have more pages with a longer list of names hidden somewhere?" he drawled.

"Six women. Four years." She shrugged. And fought back the hot blast of embarrassment from staining her cheeks. "It does seem a little on the thin side."

"When you're a man in my position, you can't afford to be reckless with women. Especially when your father was a whore." He chuckled. "Come now, Sophie," he mocked. "You didn't come across that bit of information in all of your research?" Oh yes, she had. But her poker face must've been woefully inadequate because he arched a dark brow and downed the rest of the alcohol in his glass in one gulp. Setting the glass on the bar behind him, he cocked his head to the side, a razor-sharp half smile tilting the corner of his mouth. "Of course you did," he murmured. "Well, don't leave me in suspense. Tell me what you dug up on Vernon Lowell's propensity for adultery."

"Joshua," she whispered, her mind, her traitorous heart rebelling at engaging in this.

Not for his father's sake? No, Vernon had been the whore his son had called him. She didn't want to go there for Joshua's sake. Because underneath that taunting, I-don't-give-a-damn tone, his pain echoed like a distant foghorn warning of upcoming danger.

"Don't stop now." The smile sharpened. "Do tell."

Inhaling a breath, she held it. Then slowly released

it. He wasn't going to let this go. For some reason, he appeared in a masochistic mood, and was using her as his weapon of choice.

"Vernon was known to have a…" She hesitated, searching those gold-flecked hazel eyes. "Roving eye," she finished. Lamely.

"He fucked anything in a skirt." The bald, flat statement crashed between them like shattered glass. "That is what you were so diplomatically trying to say, correct? He was an unfaithful bastard who betrayed his marriage vows on a regular basis and didn't care if his wife found out. And she did find out. My mother always knew when he found a new mistress. And we—Jake, Oliver and I—all knew because they weren't quiet about arguing over it."

Surprise rippled through her. Vernon had married up when he'd wed his wife. Eve Evans-Janson had been a society daughter with a pedigree that dated past colonial times. Her connections had opened many doors for him. Most people would consider her rather plain in the beauty department, but Sophie had always thought her loveliness exceeded mere looks. From pictures and her own memories, she remembered the other woman carrying herself like a queen. Dignified. Proud. So why would a woman like her accept a husband who cheated so openly without care for her feelings?

"Why would she—"

"Put up with a man who not only couldn't, but wouldn't, keep it in his pants?" he finished in a derisive drawl. "Simple. Comfort. Money. Even though my father did whatever he wanted and refused to give her the one thing she desperately wanted—a daughter—she stayed with him because divorce was embarrassing. Reputation and the image of a perfect marriage and family were vital to her. So she looked the other way in public and cried and raged in private. And… Despite all his selfishness, she loved him. Desperately."

Sadness coiled around her heart and squeezed hard. She should be outraged on his mother's behalf—even angry with her for settling. For not demanding more for herself, for her children. But… Hadn't she been Eve at one time? Hadn't she loved a man so completely she'd been willing to ignore her instincts, look the other way, almost ignore her ethics? The only difference between her and Joshua's mother was she finally walked away and refused to lose her independence to another man again.

Another of those serrated barks of laughter echoed in the room, and Joshua raked a hand through his hair, disheveling the thick blond strands.

"God, why in the hell am I telling you this?" he snarled, turning away from her and stalking across the floor to the window.

The "of all people" didn't need to be said. It bounced off the glass walls, deafening in its silence.

She tried not to flinch. Tried not to allow the hurt to filter through. Tried…and failed.

"I'm not your enemy," she said to his wide back.

His shoulders tensed, but he didn't face her. "And I'm sorry if I implied that you were like your father.

I didn't intend to." How to explain it'd just shocked her that such a virile, intense man who oozed power and sexuality had been intimate with only six women in four years? Hell, that didn't even average out to two a year. But given his history, the depths of which she hadn't known until this moment, she understood.

Sighing, she traced his steps and paused beside him, staring out over the beautiful view of Falling Brook at night. Houses, large and small, sprinkled among the trees and interconnecting map of streets, glittering like fairy lights. From this height, the town appeared almost magical. Serene. Made it seem as if they were hundreds of miles away instead of just several floors up.

"What do you see when you look out there?" she asked softly.

Tension and a cauldron of emotion continued to emanate from him, but when he replied, it was just as quietly. "A reminder."

"Of what?" It required everything in her not to glance at him, but to keep her gaze trained on the vista stretched out before them.

"Of why I do this." *Do what? What's* this? The questions bombarded her mind, but she forcibly held her tongue. And her patience was rewarded. "Why I continue to run a company I didn't ask for in the first place. Live this life that was my father's and not my own. For the last fifteen years, I've given it and Black Crescent everything—my dedication, my time, my loyalty, my goddamn soul. And in return? In return, I have a shade of a mother who I am powerless to help.

My brothers don't speak to me because they hate who I've become a reflection of. My father is still MIA, and I have no idea whether he is dead or alive. And no matter how hard I work, how many hours I put in, how much money I bring in to repay those robbed and devastated by my father, it's never enough. I'll always be looked at with suspicion, judged for having the same blood in my veins as a criminal."

Her palms itched to touch him. To slide between him and the glass, smooth her hands up his hard chest and strong neck to cup his jaw between them. To, in some way, assume the pain that he wouldn't allow himself to show. But she caught herself, nonetheless. The sheer magnetism of this man dominated any room he stood in. Yet... How could anyone, after spending time with him, not see the emotions that roiled beneath that austere surface like water just under a boil?

"There's this gaping hole in my life," he continued in that gravel-and-midnight-silk voice. "And it doesn't matter what I do, I can't fill it. I don't know *how* to fill it." He shook his head, and he scoffed. "And the funniest, most pathetic part? When you first told me I might have a daughter, a part of me was thrilled. Because it meant that my life hadn't been a waste. That I had a purpose other than rebuilding the legacy my father nearly destroyed. That I would be more than Vernon Lowell's son. I would be someone's father."

"You're not your father," she contradicted him, taken aback at her own vehemence. Even more so at the knell of truth that bloomed in her chest...deeper.

Somewhere between the meeting where he agreed to take her help and finding that list of names, she came to believe him about not knowing he had a child out there. Or even if the child from the DNA report was his. She released a trembling breath, spreading her hand over her suddenly tumbling stomach. "You're not Vernon," she repeated, stronger, firmer.

And maybe he heard the belief in her voice. Because he finally looked at her, his green-and-gold eyes burning down into her. Straight through her.

"You're sure about that?" he ground out. But before she could answer, he turned fully toward her, his palm flattening on the glass above her head. "You were the one who accused me of denying my illegitimate child's existence. Of carrying on and not caring that I had fathered a baby and left it out there somewhere for her and her mother to cope on their own."

Yes, she had. Regret eddied inside her, and she briefly closed her eyes against the oily, slick slide of it. Her article had dragged the scandal out of the past, buffed it up and placed it out all shiny and new for people to feast on again. She had a direct hand in him standing here, surrounded by a darkness that seemed ravenous and ready to swallow him whole.

Her fault. So at least, she owed him the truth. Her truth. Even if he could give two shits about it.

"It's true," she murmured, tipping her head back and meeting his piercing gaze. "I did believe that. But that was before I knew you—"

"You don't know me," he growled.

"That's where you're wrong," she objected, shifting into his space. Surprise flared in his eyes, flecks of gold brightening. But then his lids lowered, gaze becoming hooded and hiding his thoughts. His reaction. But it didn't stop her from claiming another inch. If she took a deep breath, her breasts would brush the wide, solid wall of his chest. The tips of her shoes nudged his, and his scent, so earthy, so virile, so delicious, enveloped her, and she battled the pull of it. For now. "You might be several things—ruthless, proud, arrogant, rude and at times so cold I'm afraid you'll leave burn marks on my skin—but you aren't a deadbeat father. You would never force a child to suffer what you have. Much less one who belonged to you."

He didn't move; his chest didn't even rise and fall on ragged breaths. Like hers did.

"So you're wrong," she said, surrendering to her earlier need and reaching for him. His hand shot out, quick as a snake, and encircled her wrist, his grip firm but not bruising. The dominance of his hold throbbed low in her belly. Her heart thudded against her sternum, but not in fear. Excitement. Need. They both streamed through her, one a sizzling current, the other fierce and liquid hot.

Testing him—pushing him—she lifted her other hand, cupping his face and half expecting him to evade her. But he didn't. He remained still, rigid. Yet, he let her hand mold to the blade of his jaw and the hollow of his cheek. The bristle of his five o'clock shadow abraded her skin, and she logged it as another sensory memory to hoard and savor.

"I know you better than anyone else. More than the people who only see what you permit them to. More than the brothers who left you to fix what was so broken. More than the women you've allowed to touch your body." She traced the curve of his bottom lip with her fingertips. "Does that scare you, Josh?"

She deliberately used the shortened version of his name, increasing the charged intimacy snapping between them like a loose live wire.

With a low rumble, he cuffed her other hand, trapping it against his mouth. His teeth sank into the fleshy heel of her palm, and her groan rolled out of her, unbidden and unrestrained. The flick of his tongue against the same flesh, as if soothing it of the tiny sting, drew another moan from her, this one softer...hungrier.

"No, you don't scare me, Sophie," he said, nipping again at her. "Because that would mean you had the power to hurt me. And I don't trust you enough to give you that power." Tugging on her wrist, he eliminated the negligent amount of space separating them, and she shivered as her breasts crushed his chest, her thighs pressed against his. His erection nestled against her belly. Whatever air remained in her lungs evaporated into vapor at the evidence of his arousal. For her. All for her. "But I want you. As much of a goddamn idiot it makes me, I want to fuck you until your voice is raw from screaming my name. Until you come around me, squeezing me so hard that my dick is bruised. Until my body aches from giving both of us what we need."

Oh. God. Each erotic word stuck her like tiny blows, her sex clenching over and over. Begging for the carnal image he drew. Pleading to be filled, taken, branded. She trembled, harder this time, thankful for the hard body and grips on her hands that held her up.

But doubts and threads of fear wound their way through the fiercely pounding desire. If she were smart, if she'd truly learned from the past, she would halt this…this thing with Joshua before it went any further. At the very least, she could be in danger of losing her job for a serious conflict of interest if anyone found out about this. But not even her career trumped the very real terror of being that woman she'd been with Laurence. Her love for him had turned her into someone she hadn't known, dependent on his approval, his affection, his attention. She'd almost lost everything over him—her career, her future, herself.

She wasn't in love with Joshua, though. The lust turning her into this clawing, biting sexual creature demanding to be satisfied was unprecedented, but that was physical. Chemical. Not emotional.

As long as she kept her fickle, hardheaded heart out of this, she could give her body what it craved and protect herself.

"One night," she said, almost wincing at the note of desperation in her voice. And how he, again, went still, that multihued stare boring into her. But neither made her rescind the condition. "One night," she repeated. "No strings. No expectations. Just two people beating back their demons together."

God, why had she said that last part? It revealed too much.

And Joshua didn't ignore it. Releasing her wrists, he cupped the nape of her neck with one hand and cradled her hip with the other. Holding her. Steadying her. And because it would be only for the night, she allowed herself to lean into his strength. To depend on it.

"You have demons, Sophie?" he murmured, his gaze roaming her face as if already searching out the answer for himself rather than trust her to give an honest answer to him.

Smart man.

"Don't we all?" she countered, and it would've been flippant if not for the rasp betraying the power of hers.

"I'll exorcise them," he growled, pulling her impossibly closer. "We'll exorcise them together."

His mouth crushed hers.

On a whimper, she willingly, eagerly parted her lips for the sweet and wild invasion of his tongue. Impatiently twisted hers around his, dueling, parrying, meeting him thrust for thrust, stroke for stroke. With her hands free, she fisted the lapels of his tuxedo jacket, not caring that she was wrinkling the clothes that no doubt had cost thousands. Nothing mattered except the taste of him, the power of him, the raw passion he whipped to a frenzy in her.

Greedy for more, she rose to her tiptoes, the stilettos she still wore aiding in the endeavor. She opened wider for him, silently demanding he take more, give her more. The hand on her nape shifted upward, tunneling through her hair, twisting, tugging. Tiny pinpricks danced across her scalp, and every one of them echoed in a path down her spine, settling in the small of her back. Restless, she slid her hands up his chest, over his shoulders and into his shorter hair. Clutching the strands, she held him to her, drowning in this kiss that should be either illegalized or memorialized.

Joshua tore his mouth from hers, trailing a scorching path over her chin and down her throat, licking and sucking. She slicked the tip of her tongue over her kiss-swollen lips, savoring the flavor of him on her. Teeth scraped over her collarbone, and she tipped her head to the side, granting him easier access. Her lashes fluttered, lowering, and she basked in each gloriously wicked sensation.

And yet, it wasn't enough.

An urgent need to touch bare skin—his bare skin—riding her, she released him to dive her hands beneath his tuxedo jacket and shove it over his shoulders and down his arms. He straightened, staring down at her from beneath a hooded gaze, letting her strip him. Unable to meet it, she dipped her head, focusing on loosening the buttons down the front of his dress shirt. And as she revealed inch after inch of taut golden skin, all traces of awkwardness vanished. She sighed, fingers slightly shaking, anticipation soaring through her. When she pushed the last button through its corresponding hole, she placed her palms on his corrugated abs, her sigh transforming into a dark, low moan at first contact of skin to skin.

Jesus, did the man harbor a furnace in his big body? Heat simmered underneath her hands, skating up her arms, over her chest and tightening her nipples beneath her dress before flowing farther south to culminate between her wet, trembling thighs. She squeezed them together and shuddered as it only increased the aching emptiness. The desperate need.

"You're so beautiful," she breathed, stroking up his chest and under the open sides of the shirt, slowly peeling it, too, from his body so it tumbled to the floor with his jacket. "Like a work of art."

She stiffened as soon as the words tumbled from her lips and jerked her gaze from his magnificent form to his face. But if her slip caused him any pain, he didn't show it. Or maybe, in this place where they were baring the bodies and just a little bit of themselves, the thought of his former passion didn't bother him.

Or maybe she was assigning more importance, more intimacy to this night of sex than it warranted.

Regardless, he deserved to be admired. To be worshipped. Smooth, tight skin stretched across wide shoulders and chest and down over a flat, ridged stomach. Brown hair dusted across his pecs and narrowed to a silken line that bisected the ladder of abs. Twin grooves lined both hips, disappearing beneath the waistband of his pants. Heeding the call and invitation of that delineated arrow, she followed the lines with her fingertips, dipping beneath the band...

"Slow down," Joshua ordered in a sharp voice that carried a bit of a snap. He emphasized the command by grabbing her wrists and, turning her with his body, pressed her back against the window. Transferring both of her wrists to one hand, he lifted her arms above her head, caging them against the cool glass, as well. It didn't stop her from twisting in his grip, arching toward him. Rolling her hips over the prominent thickness tenting the front of his slacks. "Dammit, Sophie," he growled.

Then, with a jerk that left her breathless, he yanked down her dress, exposing her breasts to the air, his glittering gaze and, *oh God*, his mouth.

She cried out, her knees close to collapsing as he sucked so hard on her, the pull of it resonated high and deep in her sex. Could she orgasm just from this? Before Joshua, she would've scoffed at the idea of it, but with his tongue curling around her nipple, flicking it, drawing on it—she was a convert. Especially with her feminine flesh spasming, her hips bucking, seeking to grind that same flesh over him...

"Josh," she pleaded, tugging against his hold. "Please. Let me touch you." Yes, she was begging. And didn't care.

He loosened his grip, and she immediately took advantage, clutching his shoulders, digging her nails into the dense muscle. His grunt of pleasure fueled her on, and she raked a path down his back, then surrendered to the need to just...hold him.

Wrapping an arm around his shoulders and the other around his head, she embraced him, savoring the heat of him, the power of him even as he continued to sensually torment her flesh. Tipping her head back against the glass, she released another cry when he switched breasts, treating it to the same attention as its twin. Big, clever fingers plucked at and pinched the damp tip his lips didn't surround. He was driving her crazy. And damn if she wasn't enjoying the trip.

"No, don't stop." The plea escaped her along with a whimper when he dragged his mouth from her breasts down her stomach. She burrowed her fingers through his hair, cradling his head, attempting to pull him back.

"Not done, sweetheart," he murmured, straightening to swing her up in his arms. Once more rendering her lungs incapable of taking in air with both the show of strength and the softly spoken endearment.

They didn't go far. Just across the room to the dark freestanding fireplace. He lowered her back to the floor and, in seconds, had her side zipper down, the dress gone, and leaving her clothed in a skimpy black thong and silver heels. Her toes curled inside her shoes. For several long, charged moments, he stared down at her, his eyes more brown than green. Lust burned in them, throwing more kindling on the same fire razing her to the ground.

"Why do you hide this gorgeous body under those clothes," he ground out, his fingers flexing next to his thighs. "But if I'd known those conservative shirts covered these perfect breasts and lovely nipples... Or had a clue those knee-length skirts slid over these sweet little curves—" he slid a hand over her hip "—and legs created for squeezing a man's hips tight… Or how pretty and wet you would be—" he cupped her, and she swallowed a small scream at the possessive touch "—I would've had you up on my desk the first day you walked into my office, pretty much telling me to go screw myself. Did you know I wanted you then, Sophie? That I was picturing you laid out on top of my files and spreadsheets, your thighs wide, letting me pound inside you until everyone on the other side of that door knew that I was taking you, owning every scream and cry? Owning you?"

Shock rippled through her. At his explicit words and that he'd wanted her as far back as when she'd charged into his office. A tenderness that had no place between them tried to infiltrate the lust, but she battled it back. Self-preservation. She had to keep this about the sex.

Joshua didn't give her an opportunity to respond— if she'd been able to anyway—because he knelt between her legs. After whisking off her shoes, he stroked his hands up her calves, over her knees and palmed her inner thighs. Her breath, loud in her own ears, soughed in and out of her chest as she waited for him to graze the swollen, damp flesh covered by black lace. Air whispered over her but did nothing to cool the heat building inside her, stoked by his words and caresses.

His fingertips danced over her, and with a mewl that would probably embarrass her later, she rocked into the too-light but too-much touch. Sensitive and so deprived, her sex clenched hard, sending a spasm through her. She was ready to beg, to write a freaking formal entreaty, if he would only give her what her body literally wept for when he tugged aside the soaked panel of her panties and plunged a thick, long finger inside her.

She screamed.

And shattered. The release swept through her, over her, the pinched quality of it bordering on pain. It was good. So good. But still not enough. Even as the final waves of orgasm ebbed, the need returned, brewing underneath the blissed-out lethargy.

With a snarl curling his lips, Joshua yanked her panties down her useless legs and spread her wide for him. He dived into her, his mouth covering her still-quivering flesh, his tongue curling around the pulsing button of nerves cresting her mound. He growled against her, the sound vibrating against her, shoving her closer to sensory overload. He lapped at her, sucked, feasted on her in a way that should've been lewd, but instead was hot as hell.

"Josh." His name burst from her, a half shout, half whimper. Pleasure ratcheted from simmering to full-out conflagration. Her fingers drove into his hair, gripping his head, holding him to her. Pushing him away.

Too much.

Oh God, not enough.

He had to stop.

She'd kill him if he dared to stop.

If her mind was conflicted, her body knew what it wanted. What it craved. Her hips bucked and rolled under his mouth, urging him on. Demanding he give her everything he had. And as her lower back tightened and tingled in that telltale sign of impending orgasm, she gasped. Never, as in *never*, had she come more than once. She didn't think it possible for her. But the jerking of her hips, the shaking of her limbs, belied that belief, proving that she just needed the right partner to bring her to the brink of pleasure—and surpass it.

No. Not the right partner.

Joshua.

Another scream built in her throat, scratching its way up when he pulled away. Leaving her aching, throbbing, *hurting* on the edge of release.

"What?" she rasped. "Please." The two words were all she could manage, lust and an aborted orgasm confusing her.

Above her, Joshua surged to his feet. He snatched his wallet from his pants and tossed it on the floor next to her shoulder. In seconds, he wrenched his pants, shoes and socks from his big body, leaving him standing extraordinarily, unbearably beautiful before her. Joshua clothed in suits and tuxedos was gorgeous. Naked, stripped of all signs of civility, was…devastating.

As if drawn to him by an invisible thread, she sat up, rising to her knees, settling her palms on lean, powerfully muscled thighs that flexed under her palms. She sighed, sliding them up the defined columns… reaching for the thick, heavy, long length of him.

"No." His long fingers caught her hand before she

could touch him. He knelt between her legs again, pressing her palm to his mouth and placing a searing openmouthed kiss there. "If I let you get your hand on me, this would be over quick. And, sweetheart, when I come, I plan to do it buried balls deep inside you, not on these pretty fingers."

He leaned over her, grabbing his wallet and removing a square foil packet. Quickly, he ripped it open and sheathed himself, then, *thank God*, he was over her, his erection nudging her entrance. Slowly pressing into her. Stretching her. Burning her.

Branding her.

Pain and pleasure mixed in a wicked, confusing blend that sent quakes rippling through her.

"Shh," Joshua crooned, brushing a kiss over her cheekbone, temple and, finally, lips. "Easy, sweetheart. You can take me. All of me." Until his reassurances, she hadn't been aware of the whimpers spilling from her or the restless shifting to get closer, to back away… She didn't know. The pressure of his possession… It filled her almost to overflowing. It overwhelmed her.

For a stark second, panic seized her. In this moment, she felt owned. Not just herself anymore. With him planted so deep inside her, she didn't belong to herself—she belonged to him. To them.

"Look at me, Sophie," he murmured, the soft tone carrying an underlying vein of steel. She couldn't help but obey and opened her eyes to meet his. Golden flames burned in a nearly dark brown field, scorching her. "Do you have any idea how you feel to me? So wet, tight like the most brutal fist but utterly fucking perfect surrounding me, squeezing me. Holding me. It's the sweetest hell. I might be covering you... I might be so goddamn deep I don't know if I can find my way out... But you have the control here. The power. So what are you going to do with me, Sophie? What are you going to do with us?"

His corded arms bracketed her head, and he held his large frame suspended above her, a very fine tremor running through him and belying the gentleness of his voice. And his words. God, they seeped into her, heating her, relaxing her tense muscles, dulling the edges of pain until only the pleasure of his dominance, his possession remained.

She released her grip on his upper arms and, sliding her hands up and over his shoulders, wound her arms around his neck, pulling him down for a slow, raw kiss.

"I'm going to take you. I'm going to wreck us," she whispered against his lips.

Hunger, dark and fierce, flashed in his gaze, but also delight flared bright and quick. Claiming control of the kiss, he pulled free from her body, then sank back inside, dragging a soft cry from her. Lifting her legs, she wrapped them around his waist, and he hissed, surging deeper. Filling her more. Thrust for thrust, she met him, taking him just as she promised. Wrecking them with each roll of her hips, each wet, voracious kiss, each scratch of her nails and whispered demand for "more, harder."

Carnal. Wild. Hot.

Joshua rode her hard, granting her no mercy. He

buried himself inside her over and over, setting off sizzling currents with each drag of his cock through her channel. She cried out with the intensity of the pleasure, from the onslaught of it. Twisting and writhing beneath him, she chased the orgasm that loomed so close.

"Josh," she pleaded, desperate, greedy.

"Give it to me, Sophie," he ground out. "Come for me."

He palmed one of her thighs, spreading her wider, lifting her into his thrusting body. Sliding the other hand down between her breasts, he didn't stop until he circled the nerve-packed nub nestled between her folds. Thrust. Circle. Thrust. Circle.

The scream ripped from her throat as she exploded. For a moment, she fought against the release, afraid of the sheer ferocity and wildness of it. But it swelled stronger, swamping her, threatening to break her. Then reshape her into someone she was afraid she'd no longer recognize.

Closing her eyes, she surrendered.

Seven

Joshua stared at his computer monitor, but just like the previous hour, the report from his chief financial officer remained a blurred jumble of numbers.

"Dammit." Disgusted, he threw his pen down on his desk and shot to his feet. His chair rolled back, bumping against the bookcase behind it.

He scrubbed a hand down his face, then wrapped it around the back of his neck. Massaging the tense muscles there, he strode to the floor-to-ceiling window and stared out. Usually, the sight of the parking lot full of his employees' cars sent a surge of satisfaction spiraling through him. There'd been a time after he'd taken over Black Crescent when the lot had been almost empty. Only he, Haley and a few other loyal staff members had remained when the company fell apart. Those days had been…grim. Though he'd kept up a stalwart front for everyone, he'd been terrified. Of failing to rebuild the company and paying back the families his father had devastated. Of letting down those few who'd still believed in and trusted him when his father hadn't given them a reason to.

Of proving those who'd condemned him with "like father, like son" right.

His father. It always came back to him.

But it wasn't Vernon who had him distracted and unable to concentrate this Monday morning. How easy it would be to place the blame on him instead of *her*.

Sophie.

As if just the thought of her name jammed open a door he'd padlocked shut, images from Saturday night rushed through his head, a ceaseless stream of erotic snapshots.

Sophie, hips rolling and bucking to meet his devouring mouth as he held her thighs spread wide for him.

Sophie, twisting and undulating beneath him, voice cracking as she begged him to possess her harder.

Sophie, body arched tight, beautiful breasts pointed toward the ceiling, eyes glazed with pleasure as she came so hard it required every bit of his tattered control to prevent immediately following her.

Sophie, curled up against his side, her head resting on his shoulder, her soft, even breath caressing his damp skin. Her small, delicate hand splayed wide on his chest.

If the mental flashes of her uninhibited passion had his body hardening and arousal clenching his gut, then it was the memory of her cuddled into his body, sleeping so trustingly, that had a vise grip squeezing his heart.

And that grip unnerved him.

One night. No strings. That had been their agreement. The reasons for it—for him, at least—hadn't changed come the morning when they dressed in silence and he drove her home.

She was a reporter who had just done a story on him and his family. How he'd let his guard down Saturday night and confessed his unhappiness about his life and the jacked-up state of his family even before the scandal still astonished him. That—his penchant to reveal things he'd never told another soul—was her superpower. And his downfall. He'd basically handed her information for her follow-up on him, and if she did write it, he had no one to blame but himself.

What was it about this woman that made him so vulnerable? That had him ignoring every self-protective instinct?

He couldn't do that again. Couldn't afford to. Couldn't afford to open Black Crescent up to any more controversy and couldn't afford to let her in. To open his heart.

Everyone he'd ever loved had abandoned him. His father with going on the lam. His mother by mentally leaving him. His brothers by withdrawing from him, then icing him out of their lives.

No, if she hadn't set the limits on their one night of the hottest sex he'd ever had or believed possible, then he would've.

"Joshua, I've been buzzing you," Haley announced from behind him. He pivoted sharply, bemused. He'd been so deep in thought he hadn't heard the phone intercom or his assistant enter his office. "Where were you just now?"

He shook his head, slicing a hand through the air to wave away her question. "Just going over my eleven o'clock appointment with Clark Reynolds from Venture Investments. What'd you need?"

Haley tilted her head, studying him through a narrowed gaze. She didn't outright accuse him of lying, but the speculation in her hazel eyes did. "Nice try. But deflection has never worked with me. Are you sure you weren't just mooning over Sophie Armstrong?"

He snorted, striding back toward his desk. "I've never mooned a day in my life."

"I know. And that's your problem."

"My problem?" He sank into his chair. "I wasn't aware I had one. Well, other than a bossy executive assistant who doesn't know when to let stuff go."

"Oh, you have one," she drawled, folding into the armchair across from his desk. Leaning forward, her dark blond eyebrows drew together in a frown. "When was the last time your life didn't revolve around this company, the employees or paying back the families affected by the scandal?"

"Haley," Joshua said, stiffening. "I don't—"

"I know you don't want to talk about it. You never do," she cut him off. "That's another problem. You might be the savior of Black Crescent, Josh, but that's not all you are. You deserve more. You deserve to have time to yourself, take a vacation. Leave this place at a decent hour. Have a private life. Yes, you've had relationships in the past, but when was the last time you just let yourself fall for someone? Let them interfere with your carefully regimented schedule and order? Let them make your life messy with laughter and love? I know the answer to all those questions. Never."

Joshua clenched his jaw, trapping the heated words that threatened to burst free. He didn't want to hurt her feelings. Haley might be his assistant, but she was also family. Like his younger sister. But this topic was off-limits. "Haley, I don't want to hurt your feelings. But this is—"

"None of my business, I know. But this—" she stood and set down the tablet she held on the desk, sliding it toward him "—makes it everyone's business."

He stared at her for several moments before dropping his gaze to the screen. His irritation evaporated, dissolved by shock.

Pictures from Saturday night's art gala. Some depicted him and other partygoers, including the redhead he'd been seated next to at dinner, who'd propositioned him with a nightcap after the event. Those images didn't ensnare his attention or had his heart pounding like an anvil against his chest. Didn't have desire flaming bright and hot inside him.

The photograph of Sophie, so beautiful in the silver strapless gown that had molded to her slim figure and highlighted every curve, and him standing outside the museum had him battling back the surge of lust brewing low in his stomach.

Unlike with the redhead, he'd lost the polite but aloof mask he usually donned at those occasions. Though a small distance separated them, he stared down at her with an intensity—a hunger—that was anything but polite. And Sophie, head tipped back, exhibited a vulnerability that he immediately hated the photographer for capturing.

He tore his gaze away from the image and scanned the caption underneath.

Black Crescent Hedge Fund CEO Joshua Lowell and mystery guest...or date? Could it be the famous—or infamous—businessman is finally settling down?

Flicking a glance to the top of the page, he glimpsed the name of the site. And fisted his fingers next to the tablet. A notorious gossip website that focused on dishing dirty on high society. If he had a dollar for every time his or his family's names had been mentioned in this column, he'd have been able to compensate the bankrupted families years ago, and with interest.

Dammit. Had Sophie seen this? Possibly not. She

might be a reporter, but she was also an investigative journalist. Not some gossipmonger.

"What's going on between you and Sophie Armstrong?" Haley asked softly.

He jerked his head up, having momentarily forgotten she stood across from him. "Nothing. She happened to attend the same gala as I did, and we were leaving at the same time. She wasn't my date."

"The columnist mentioned you two left together. That she got into your car," Haley persisted.

Dammit. Anger pulled hard and tight inside him. Fucking media. "I gave her a ride home since we were both headed back to Falling Brook. End of story." If the end of the story included his driving into Sophie's sweet body on a rug that he wouldn't ever be able to walk by again without seeing her coming apart on it.

Haley silently studied him again, her scrutiny too seeing, too knowing. "Neither of your faces say 'casual acquaintance' or 'friendly ride home.'" Before he could snarl a reply, she continued, voice soft, "And I'm glad."

He frowned, taken aback. "You're glad my privacy was invaded and I'm now a topic of speculation and gossip? Again."

Haley straightened, a flicker of emotion rippling across her face. But before he could decipher it, she arched an eyebrow, her eyes direct and unwavering. "No, I'm positively delighted that someone has managed to get through that thick layer of 'back the hell off' that you've wrapped yourself in these past fifteen years. I'm happy that you've found someone that you would let down your guard long enough to be captured by some random photographer. Because whether or not you want to admit it—or are ready to admit it—she *is* important to you. Now I'm just praying that you don't mess it up by pushing her away."

She turned away and strode across his office and left, closing the door behind her with a quick snick. But her warning reverberated in the room like a report of a gunshot.

I'm just praying that you don't mess it up by pushing her away.

Mess it up? Push her away?

He'd have to let her in first.

And that wasn't happening. Ever.

Eight

What the hell am I doing here?

The question ricocheted off Joshua's skull as he sat in the back seat of his Lincoln town car outside Sophie's apartment building. Showing up here after the photo of them on the gossip site didn't rank among his smartest decisions. If anyone saw him here, it would only feed the fires of speculation. But he'd tried to call her to see if she'd seen it and give her a heads-up if she hadn't. Either she hadn't seen his phone call or she'd refused to answer, because he hadn't been able to reach her.

Logic argued that he leave it alone—leave her alone. But the thought of her being blindsided… Well, here he was sitting outside her home like some kind of goddamn stalker. Growling a curse, he shoved open the back door.

"John, I'll give you a call when I'm finished here," he instructed his driver.

The younger man behind the wheel nodded. "Yes, sir."

Closing the door shut, he stalked across the street and up to the two-story brick building with its neat side lawns and sidewalk bordered by honeysuckle. Just as he approached the door, a couple with a small child pushed through the entrance.

"Oops, sorry 'bout that," the man apologized with a grin. "This one's a little anxious to hit the park."

"No, no, it's fine," Joshua said, stepping out of the way and catching the door before it could close.

But his gaze remained ensnared by the little girl who couldn't have been older than four years old. The same age the child Sophie accused him of having was supposed to be. A sudden longing jerked hard in his chest, catching him by surprise. Years ago, when the world had been his to conquer, he'd wanted what this husband and father had—family.

Now? Now, a wife, a child… They just meant a person had more to lose.

Shaking his head, he moved into the large lobby, letting the door close behind him. An elevator ride later, he stood in front of Sophie's apartment. Before he could again question the wisdom of being here, he knocked. And waited. And knocked again.

Hell. He glanced down at his watch: 6:48 p.m. She should've been home by now, but then again, Sophie had the same work ethic as he did. It was one of the things he admired about her despite her choice of career. So she very well could still be at the office.

He had turned and taken a step away from her door when it opened.

"Sophie," he greeted, running his gaze from the brown-and-gold wavy strands that fell over the shoulders of a purple slouchy T-shirt that hung off one shoulder, down the black leggings to her bare feet with pink-painted toes. Dragging his perusal back up, he couldn't look at her—not those slender, toned thighs, high, firm breasts or lovely dove-gray eyes—without thinking of how she'd looked, naked and damp from sweat, under him.

"Joshua, what are you doing here?" Joshua, not Josh, as she'd called him for most of those hot, dark hours they'd spent together.

Part of him wanted to demand she call him the shortened version again. And in that sex-drenched, husky voice. Instead, he slid his hands in his pants pockets and kept a careful distance between them.

"I needed to talk with you about something. I'm sorry for dropping by unannounced, but you weren't answering your phone today."

"Yes." She thrust a hand through her hair, drawing the strands away from her face. "I saw the missed calls. I intended to call you back but just got really busy."

He cocked his head. "You make a shitty liar, Sophie."

She dropped her arm, heaving a sigh. "What are you doing here, Joshua?" she repeated.

"I need to talk to you. And not out here in the hallway."

"I—" Indecision flicked in her eyes, her full lips flattening. Finally, after a brief hesitation, she nodded and stepped back. "Fine. Only for a minute, though. I'm working."

Suspicion flared quick and hot in his chest. Was she writing the follow-up article on him? On what he'd revealed to her? He hadn't stipulated that Saturday night had been off the record. Would she...?

He snuffed the thoughts out as he entered her apartment and closed the door behind him. But the embers of doubt... He couldn't extinguish them. How messed up was it that he harbored reservations about her trustworthiness, but he still wanted her with a hunger that gave him stomach pains?

"Can I get you something? I was about to fix a cup of coffee. But I have wine or a bottle of water," Sophie said.

The reluctance in her offer had a corner of his mouth quirking into a humorless half smile. Good manners probably had her extending the courtesy instead of truly wanting him to stick around and enjoy a drink.

So he accepted.

"Coffee is fine."

Again, her lips tightened, but she headed to the kitchen that was separated from the living room by a breakfast bar. Taking the opportunity, he surveyed the apartment. Though on the small side, the living room with its overstuffed couches, wood coffee and end tables and big arched windows appeared cozy rather than cramped. Lived in. Compared with his condo, her place was a home, not a place to just crash instead of the office sofa.

The room flowed into a space that could've been a dining area but Sophie had jammed with filled-to-overflowing bookcases, a tiny love seat and lamps. A reading nook. Easily he could imagine her curled up on those cushions, book in hand.

He tore his gaze away, returning it to her as she finished up the second coffee in the one-cup brewer. Though irritation practically vibrated off her petite frame, her movements were fluid, graceful.

"What are you working on?" he asked, needing to remind himself of who she was. What she did. What she was capable of.

"The follow-up article from my visit to Black Crescent. I need to have it in by the end of the week."

There it was. The reminder. Ice trickled through his veins. Yes, he'd invited her into the inner sanctum of his company and revealed the programs that were close to his heart, but now, tiny pinpricks of doubts stabbed at him over that decision.

"What?" Sophie propped a hip against the counter and crossed her arms over her chest. "Having second thoughts? *You* asked *me* to Black Crescent, remember? This time I didn't force my way in," she drawled.

"I don't need any help remembering…anything," he said, and yes, it made him an asshole to feel hot satisfaction well in him as slashes of red painted her high cheekbones. But he didn't care. Not when she couldn't hide the gleam of arousal in her eyes before abruptly turning back to the counter and the coffee cups.

"Do you take sugar or cream?" she rasped. And the sound of the slightly hoarse tone...

He barely stopped himself from stalking across the space separating them and pressing his chest to her ramrod-straight spine. From notching his hard dick just above the tempting curve of her perfect ass.

"Black," he ground out.

Seconds later, she handed him the mug with Shouldn't You Be Writing? emblazoned along the side along with a picture of a shirtless Thor and his hammer. He would've assumed the choice in cup was by accident if a smirk didn't ride the corner of her mouth.

"Cute," he drawled.

"It's one of my favorites. Nothing but the best for you," she purred, strolling past him with her own plain black mug back into the living room, where her laptop sat propped on the coffee table in front of the couch. "Not that I don't doubt my coffee is wonderful, but what are you really doing here, Joshua?"

The pointed question shoved away any vestiges of humor, and he took a sip of the steaming-hot, fragrant brew before replying. "Pictures of us together from the art gala were posted online in a society gossip column. I didn't know if you were aware. But in case you weren't, I wanted to give you a heads-up. Although you weren't named, the columnist included some speculation about our relationship to one another."

She huffed out a dry laugh. "Oh yes, I already

know about it. Althea called me into her office today and asked if anything was going on between us. She's worried about the conflict of interest for the paper if the reporter of the story on Black Crescent is involved with the CEO."

"What did you tell her?"

"I told her no, of course."

"So you lied," Joshua drawled.

If he hadn't been watching her so closely, he might've missed the slight tremble in her hand as she set her mug on the coffee table. But he didn't. And he had to battle back the urge to cross the floor, take that hand, lift it and still the shivering with his mouth.

"It wasn't a lie. There isn't anything between us. Saturday was one night. One time. That was our deal."

"And if I want to renegotiate the deal?" he murmured.

The same shock that widened her eyes reverberated through him. Where had that come from? Asking for another night—another taste of her lips, another chance to drive into that sweet little body—hadn't been his intention when he'd pulled up outside her building. *Warn her, get out.* That had been the plan. But lust had overridden common sense and hijacked his mouth. But he couldn't exist within four feet of her and not crave her. Not want a repeat of the night that was branded into his memory with startling and unnerving clarity. Maybe he just needed to convince himself that his brain had exaggerated the pleasure he experienced. That nothing could be that good in reality.

And maybe he was just seeking an excuse to get her under him again.

He still didn't trust her. Didn't 100 percent believe that she wasn't using him for another story. But none of that stopped his dick from throbbing like a toothache—insistent, hurting and needing relief.

"Joshua..." She shook her head, ducking her head as she pinched the bridge of her nose. "I don't think—"

"Look at me, Sophie," he ordered, setting his cup on the breakfast bar behind him. He moved farther into the living room, not stopping until only inches separated them. She lifted her gaze to his, and her obedience in this when she refused to give it to him anywhere else had excitement and arousal plowing through him. "Look at me and tell me that you're not already feeling my hands on you. Tell me your nipples aren't already hardening, begging for my fingers, my tongue. Tell me you're not already hot and wet for me, desperate to have me stretching you again, filling you." He grasped her chin between his thumb and forefinger, tilting her head farther back. "You can tell me all of that, Sophie, and I'll walk out of here."

Her moist, warm breath broke on her parted lips, echoing in the room. For several long moments, she stared up at him with those molten silver eyes, her slender body swaying toward his, as if seeking his warmth, his possession.

A shudder worked through her, and, lowering her lashes, she stepped back, breaking his hold on her.

Rubbing her hands up and down her arms, she turned away from him. *Give me those eyes. Look at me*, battered his tongue, needing to get out. But he clenched his teeth, trapping the command. Pride imprisoned what sounded too damn close to a plea.

"Is it so easy for you?" she whispered.

He frowned, shifting forward, reclaiming a little of the distance she'd inserted. It was an unconscious movement, as if his body couldn't stand not feeling her warmth or being wrapped in her scent.

"Is what easy for me?" he pressed.

"This." Pivoting to face him again, she waved a hand between them. "You don't trust me," she said flatly.

"No," he replied, just as blunt. "I don't."

Hurt spasmed across her face, but in the next instant her expression hardened into a cool mask that somehow appeared so wrong on her. Like an ill-fitting dress.

"Then why would you want to be with someone you believe would possibly sell you out for a story?" she scoffed, but a thin line of anger edged the question.

"A relationship with you and fucking are two different things," he said, voice hard, matter-of-fact. "And if that's what you're looking for from me, then we can end this now. I don't do long-term commitments. I'm not the man who can give you the happy home with a perfect, smiling family and well-behaved dog. But I am the man who can make you come so hard it hurts. Yes, Sophie. I'll make it hurt in the very best way," he murmured, lust gripping him so hard, so tight, he could barely draw in a breath. "I don't need to trust you for that."

Her thick fringe of lashes lowered, and her hooded silver gaze razed his skin. Red stained her cheeks and that lush mouth appeared even plumper, bitable. The aloof coldness had evaporated from her expression, leaving this one behind. And he recognized it. This face, stamped with arousal, had haunted his every waking and sleeping hour since Saturday night.

Yet, he couldn't deny glimpsing the flicker of pain beneath the lust.

Before his mind could check him, he took a step toward her to…what? Ease it? Order her to tell him how to make it disappear?

She shot a hand up, palm out, and he halted.

Thank God.

"I have my own stipulations. I don't have your trust, fine. But I will have your fidelity. While we're doing…this arrangement, you don't sleep with anyone else. Just me."

"Of course," he growled. "And the same with you. I'm the only man inside you."

"Of course," she said, throwing his words back at him with a snap. "And at any time either of us wants out, it's over." He nodded, but she continued, "One last thing. This stays here. No one else knows. Anyone finding out could cost me my job. I might be losing some of my pride entering into this with you, but I refuse to lose my career."

She murmured the last part of that almost to herself, and he scowled. What the hell did that mean? Before he could demand an explanation, though, she stuck out her hand toward him, the fingertips nudging his chest.

"Deal?" she asked.

He stared down at it, anger and wild, raw need crowding into him. Pride? Being with him stripped her of pride? What else could he strip her of?

Grasping her wrist, he tugged her hand up to his mouth. And licked the center of her palm, swirling his tongue over the soft flesh. Her gasp reverberated around them, and she tried to curl her fingers into her palm, but he stayed the motion with his other hand, holding her spread wide for him. He flicked a wet caress in between each finger before sinking his teeth into the heel of her palm.

A shudder racked her body, followed by a throaty moan that had his dick twitching.

"Joshua," she whimpered.

"Josh," he corrected, voice harsh, roughened by the hunger that gnawed at him like a voracious beast. "Say it." He trailed a finger down the elegant line of her throat, tracing the shallow dip in the middle of her collarbone.

"Josh," she whispered, and her swift capitulation was a stroke over his thick, pulsing flesh. And a caress to his pounding heart. She moved forward until her thighs bumped his and her breasts plumped against his chest. He fought to lock down the urge that howled at him to take her down to the floor and claim. Rising to the tips of her bare toes, she brought her mouth a breath away. He slid his tongue out, brushing that temptation of a full bottom lip. "Josh," she repeated, softer, huskier.

In answer, in reward, he took her mouth.

Releasing her hand, he cradled her jaw, pressing his thumb on her chin and tugging down to open her more to him. She tilted her head, complying. Breathing a snarl into her, he thrust his tongue past her lips, rubbing and twisting, coaxing her to play with him. Not that she needed any persuading. She met him, danced with him. Dared him. Nails digging into his shoulders through his suit jacket, she coiled her tongue with his, sucking hard, and the pull arrowed straight to his dick.

A savage, almost animalist burst of lust exploded within him, and he bent his knees to cup her ass in both hands and straightened, hauling her up his body. Her legs wound around his waist, her arms around his neck, settling her sex right over his erection. *Goddamn.* He clenched his molars together, reaching for his rapidly dwindling control. Still, nothing could stop him from punching his hips forward and stroking her up and down his dick. Her thin yoga pants and his slacks might as well as have been created of air. Her folds slipped over him, shooting electric pulses down his spine.

"Bedroom?" he ground out.

"Down the hall," she rasped. "Last door on the right."

In the small apartment, it didn't take long to find her room. With long, impatient strides, he entered and headed straight for the bed. Carefully, he lowered her to the floor, sliding his hands up over her hips, the indents of her waist, the sides of her breasts until he held her face in his hands. Tipping her head back, he stared into her eyes. And though desire rode him like a jockey hell-bent on leather, he paused, seeking any flicker of hesitation, of second thoughts.

"I need to hear you say it, Sophie," he said, his voice seeming to boom in the tense quiet of the bedroom. "Say you want this. You want me to touch you. You want me inside you."

He waited. And he would continue to wait. Because a part of him—the stubborn part that grief, pain and betrayal hadn't managed to amputate—*had* to hear her utter those words. Craved it like a drowning man seeking that life-giving gulp of air.

"I want this. I want you," she whispered, threading her fingers through his hair and pulling his head down until their noses bumped and her lips grazed his. "I want you to touch me. Want you so deep inside me I'll feel you tomorrow. Will you give it to me, Josh?"

He didn't answer her. At least not with words. But with his mouth, his tongue, his hands? God, yes. He dug his fingers into her hips, jerking her closer so she would have no doubts of her effect on him. Unable to help himself, he ground his cock into the softness of her belly, even as he devoured her mouth. And she held nothing back from him. Not her response, not her sexy little whimpers and cries. Had a woman ever fully let herself be so uninhibited, so vulnerable with him before?

No.

And he'd never been that way with another woman.

But with Sophie? Regardless of his claims of not trusting her, he couldn't throw up his protective shields with her. Not in this.

Here, they could be fully honest with each other. Naked in more than the baring of bodies.

Naked. As soon as the word entered his head, the longing, the greed in him intensified until it became a chant in his head.

Tearing his mouth from hers, he fisted the bottom of her T-shirt and yanked it over her head. And *oh God*. "All that time you were offering me coffee and arguing with me, you didn't have a bra on?" he snarled, palming her pretty, firm breasts and thumbing the pink nipples. Already tight, they pebbled further, and Jesus himself couldn't have stopped him from dipping his head and having a taste. And when she tugged on his hair, her groan accompanying the pricks across his scalp, he indulged himself and sucked her into his mouth, lashing the tip. Pulling free, he rubbed his lips across the beaded flesh. "If I'd known you were bare underneath that top, you would've been against the wall with my mouth on you as soon as I closed that door."

He grazed her with his teeth, wringing another cry from her. It became his mission to drag them from her, to earn a shudder from her slender frame. His mission and his pleasure.

While he switched from one breast to the other, Sophie removed his jacket, pushing it off his shoulders and arms, casting it to the floor. His shirt followed. Her nails raked down his bare back, trailing fire in their wake, and it was his turn to shiver.

Releasing her with a soft pop, he straightened, shifting forward and moving her backward until the backs of her knees hit the edge of the mattress. But at the last second, she twisted and, grabbing his upper arms, turned him. They switched positions, and she pressed her palms to his chest, her touch like live coals on his skin.

"My turn," she said, eyes so bright he swept a thumb underneath one. Then brushed his lips over the same spot. "Can't distract me," she breathed, and pushed.

He sank to the bed, his palms slapping down beside his thighs. She didn't hesitate, but knelt in front of him, and his thighs automatically spread, making room for her. His breath hitched in his lungs, and his body froze. Anticipation, lust and excitement hurtled through him, and he could only stare down at this beautiful, sensual creature as she fumbled with his thin leather belt and the closure to his pants.

The metallic grind of the zipper ricocheted through the room, deafening in his ears. She pushed the edges apart, exposing his black boxer briefs. Together, they studied the almost obscene bulge of his thick, long erection. Was she remembering the same thing as he?

How he fit inside that too-tight and too-perfect sex? How he'd had to work his way inside her, claiming her bit by bit as she softened around him, strangling his dick even as she embraced it?

Because, God, he remembered. Remembered and wanted it so bad he'd become one huge walking ache.

Finally, when she snagged the waistband, his paralysis broke. He covered her hand with his, squeezing.

"You don't have to do this, sweetheart," he rumbled, offering her an out. Even though the thought of her tongue sliding down his column nearly had him coming without one touch.

"I know I don't *have* to," she said, lifting her gaze from his cloth-covered dick to meet his. "I *want* to."

Then she was gripping him. Stroking him.

Pleasure so sharp it danced on the edge of pain seized him, and, head thrown back, palms flattened on the mattress, he strained against it.

Nothing, *fucking nothing*, had ever felt as good as this woman's hand on his cock.

Oh damn.

He stood corrected. Hot, wet warmth bathed the head, followed by gentle swipes of a tongue. His head jacked forward, *needing* to take in the sight of Sophie with her mouth full of his flesh.

Locking his muscles, he fought down the ball of fire coalescing and swirling at the base of his spine and lower. God, he was going to come. Right down her throat from just the swipe of her tongue. He closed his eyes but, seconds later, snapped them open, unable to not look. To stare. To behold this picture of knee-shaking carnality and brand it on his brain.

Lashes lowered, color painted her sharp cheek-bones and one of those hungry whimpers escaped her as she swallowed him down, tongue rubbing, mouth sucking. Her fist pumped the bottom half of his pounding column, and her damp lips bumped her fingers each time she bobbed over him. Up and down, she tortured him, loving him, making him her slave.

Because right now he would do anything for her if she. Just. Didn't. Stop.

"Sweetheart," he growled, and the endearment was churned-up gravel in his throat. "You're trying to break me with your greedy little mouth. And I'm going to let you do it. I'm going to let you take me apart."

His words seemed to galvanize her, to fuel her passion. Tunneling both hands in her hair and tangling them in the thick strands, he didn't try to control her, just allowed himself to be swept along in the ride.

She took him deeper and deeper until the tip of him nudged the back of her throat.

She let him slip into that narrow passage, swallowed around him.

She elicited shudder after shudder, curse after curse from him.

And when the telltale sizzle snapped and popped down his spine, legs to the soles of his feet and then back up to the base of his dick, he didn't hold back. Didn't pull her off him.

He gave her everything. Every last bit of him.

Chest heaving, he waited for the dark edges crowding his vision to retreat. Only then did he loosen his grasp on Sophie's head and suck in a much-needed breath into his screaming lungs. That orgasm should've destroyed him, laid him out. Instead, it fed the desire that still flowed through him like an open pipe.

He clutched her shoulders and, surging to his feet, dragged her up with him. In seconds, he had her naked on the bed and under him. He attacked her mouth, voracious. The taste of him on her tongue only inflamed him more. Snarling against her lips, he nipped the full bottom one, then treated her chin and throat to the same erotic bites.

Once more he feasted on her breasts, licking, lapping and tweaking until she writhed beneath him, those kitten mewls spilling from her. God, he loved them. Hoarded them in his head so he could replay them later when he was alone in his bed.

He shook his head, dislodging the thoughts and the sharp stab of loneliness they lugged along with them. Skimming his lips down the center of her chest, he paused to flick his tongue in the bowl of her navel, then continued until he reached his goal.

Inhaling, he trapped the musky sweet-and-tart scent of her. He jerked awake last night with this scent teasing him, tormenting him. Unable to resist the lure, he dipped his head and dived into her sex. One hand splayed wide on her lower belly to hold her down, he palmed her inner thigh with the other, granting him easy access to the flesh that he couldn't get enough of. Her scream danced around his ears as he slid his tongue through her swollen, soaked folds, circling the bud of nerves at the top of her mound. Over and over he returned to gorge on her like the delicious, addictive-feast she was.

Her thighs clamped around his head, and her fingers dug into his hair, grasping tight, and he didn't let up. Not until he pushed her right to the edge of release—and over it.

And as she still shook and gasped on the waves of pleasure, he shoved from the bed and stripped. Removing his wallet and then a condom from the billfold, he tossed his pants to the floor and climbed back onto the mattress, crawling over her. Quickly, he sheathed his rock-hard flesh in the protection, then maneuvered her until she straddled his hips. His erection surged up between them, and he swore he could feel her labored gusts of breath on the tip.

"Ride me, sweetheart," he grated, cupping her hip and fisting his dick. "Take me."

Her eyes found his, and, without breaking their visual mating, she rose over him. Then sank down on him.

He was the first to break their locked gazes. Closing his, he released a hiss as she enveloped him, slowly accepting him. Both hands gripped her hips, steadying her. She fell forward, her palms slapping his pecs. Head bent, she pulsed up and down his flesh, taking more and more of him until, finally, she was seated on top of him. And he was so deep inside her, he had to, once more, battle back the rising of his orgasm.

"Sophie," he growled, bucking his hips as if he could screw just a little bit more of himself inside her, when there was nothing left of him to give. "So tight. So wet. So damn hot. I didn't—" He cut himself off before he could utter the rest of the too-revealing sentence. He hadn't imagined how perfect she took him. How she undid him. "You good, sweetheart?" he asked, flexing again, unable to help himself.

"Yes," she breathed, crushing a kiss to his lips. "God, *yes*."

"Take me, then," he ordered. "Take us both."

Lifting off him until only the head of his dick remained, she hovered for only a second before slamming back down on him.

Moments ago, he'd thought nothing had felt as good as Sophie's mouth on him. So wrong. Watching her rise and fall above him, face saturated with lust… Having her lush, muscular core sucking at him, fluttering around him—nothing could compare to this.

Jackknifing off the bed, he sat up, burrowed his fingers in her hair and captured her mouth, swallowing each sob, each whine. Wrapping her arms around his shoulders and head, she rode him, jerking on him, hips swiveling like the most carnal of dances. She wrenched her mouth from his, tipping her head back on her shoulders, lost in the pleasure she chased. The pleasure bearing down on him like a freight train with greased wheels.

Not without her, though. He wouldn't go without her.

Reaching between them, he slid his fingers down her quivering belly to the small, swollen bundle of nerves cresting her sex. One stroke. Two. Three, and he pressed down hard.

Her core clamped down hard on him like a vise grip, feminine muscles milking him. Grabbing her hips, he held her aloft as he thrust up into her, granting her every measure of the release that shook her like a leaf in a passion-whipped storm. Only after her screams ebbed to muted whimpers did he let go, hurtling into the dark, shattering abyss of release.

As he fell, slender arms encircled him.

And he held on.

Nine

Sophie rested her head on Joshua's chest, his steady heartbeat a reassuring thud under her ear. She should move. Should order him to leave since the sex was over, and her senses had winked back online. But her limbs, weighted down by postorgasmic lethargy and wrapped around his torso and thigh, wouldn't obey. Besides, when he'd left the bed to get rid of the condom, he'd returned with a warm, wet bath cloth to clean her. After that tender and thoughtful consideration, it would be rude of her to kick him out.

Okay, and that sounded weak even to her own ears.

She might as well just admit it; she wanted him here in her bed. His weight next to hers. His heartbeat echoing in her ear.

So dangerous. She was entering such treacherous, risky territory.

Saturday night, she'd been so certain that she would be able to contain the passion between them to one night. That she could walk away unscathed.

God, she'd been so arrogant.

He'd left her singed to her soul. And days later, she still felt the burn. So much that when he'd shown up on her doorstep, she'd tried to convince herself again that she could separate physical from emotional. That she didn't need his trust. Didn't need anything but another release that left her feeling like a post-apocalyptic refugee.

Closing her eyes, she tried to block out the direction of her wayward thoughts, but that only caused a livestream of how she'd spent the last hour with Joshua. Of their own volition, her fingertips brushed her lips. And she shivered, experiencing again the fierceness of his possession.

He was the first man she'd gone down on. Had he been able to tell? No other had stirred the need to share that intimacy, to make herself so vulnerable. To give so much—her mouth, her throat…her control.

But Joshua wasn't just any man.

Somehow, he'd sneaked beneath her carefully constructed armor and touched more than her body. He'd infiltrated her heart.

Terror barreled through her as she admitted the truth to herself.

And this time, when she squeezed her eyes shut, it wasn't the erotic reel that played over the backs of her lids. It was her, alone, curled up on her couch, hurting. Her, staring at her computer screen staring at an image of Joshua with another woman on his arm. Her, crushed and lost, gazing at her apartment door, willing a knock to sound. For him to be standing on the other side.

Pain cascaded through her in a crimson shower. Pain and fear.

He'd warned her about not wanting a relationship. Straight up told her he didn't want to be in one with her or any woman. But especially not her. He might not have voiced that, but the words had been there, ringing in the room. Not a woman who might betray him or use him for a story. He would never be able to disassociate her from her job. So once more, she faced the decision—love or her career.

Well, she would be faced with that decision if he wanted her for more than sex.

Which he didn't.

But the fear went deeper than his rejection. It reached down to the core of her that dreaded becoming dependent on a man for her happiness, her security. Because when he left, where would she be?

A shell.

"That's the second sigh in as many minutes," Joshua said, his voice rumbling under her ear. He traced a meandering trail up and down her arm, and she savored his touch. Committed this relaxed version of him to memory. "What're you thinking about?"

Of how I'm foolishly falling for you even though I know you will shatter me.

"Actually, I was thinking about you." Not exactly a lie. But sharing the truth wasn't an option.

Tension invaded his body, and she hated it. "What about me?" he asked, the same stiffness coating his question.

Heaving a sigh—her third—she sat up, her hip pressed to his, drawing her knees to her chest and wrapping her arms around them. "While I was working on my follow-up article, it struck me again how much you do for those who are in your employ and this community. All without any expectation of credit or acknowledgment. It's so admirable, and if I could put all of that in bold, font size eighteen, I would. People should know that you're not just a CEO consumed with making money. You're not just another businessman with the 'rich getting richer' mentality. You actually care about people and their welfare and their success."

Joshua rose, resting his back against her headboard, the sheet he'd pulled over them pooling around his lean waist. "I don't do it for accolades or recognition, Sophic. None of that is important to me."

"Isn't it?" she whispered. His hazel gaze sharpened, narrowing on her. Though her heart lodged in the base of her throat, she pushed on. "You might not do it for public consumption, but I suspect personal acknowledgment drives you even more."

A frown creased his forehead, and anger, as well as another unidentifiable emotion, flashed in his eyes. "You have no idea what you're talking about," he snapped.

She should let it go. He obviously didn't appreciate her playing armchair therapist. Especially not from the woman he was just fucking. But she couldn't. Joshua might not want her outside this bedroom, but God, he deserved so much more than this half life he lived. He was too good a man, had sacrificed so much for family and those who had been devastated by the Black Crescent scandal. And if no one else cared enough to tell him so, to let him off the hook he'd leaped on himself, then she would.

"Maybe not. But I know what I've seen. And as I told you before, I know you." Lowering her legs, she curled them under her hips and fully faced him. "Every time you set up a new program assisting those less fortunate than you... Every time you donate to a worthy cause... Every time you make another payment in reparation to the families bankrupted by your father's actions, you attempt to erase a black mark you believe mars your name. A black mark that you didn't put there and isn't yours anyway."

"Sophie, stop," he growled, throwing the sheet back and swinging his legs over the side of the bed.

But she shot her hand out, grabbing his wrist. He could've easily shaken her grip free, but he didn't. Maybe he didn't want to hurt her, and she had no problem taking shameless advantage of that display of thoughtfulness.

She rose to her knees and crossed the small space of the bed until she knelt at his side. Tentatively, she reached for him, her hand hovering above his shoulder. Not willing to back down now, she gently touched him. He didn't jerk away, but he remained stiff, unyielding. A slash of pain lacerated her heart, but she refused to back down.

Not when his happiness could be the casualty.

"You've lived in your father's toxic shadow all these years. When do you come out of it?" she asked softly. "When do you get the chance to live in the sun in your own light?"

"That sounds like a pretty fairy tale, but there is no coming out of it for me. Not as long as my last name is Lowell."

"But what if there is? You have nothing left to prove—you've rebuilt what Vernon almost destroyed. You've repaired your family's reputation with your hard work, dedication and loyalty. You've reimbursed the families your father stole from. What more can you give? Your life…your soul?"

He scoffed, but she didn't let him accuse her of being dramatic, which she was certain had been his next comment. Before he could reply, she slid off the bed and scooped up her discarded shirt from the floor with a "Be right back. Don't move."

By the time she returned moments later with a black binder in her arms, she half expected him to be already dressed and ready to leave her apartment. He had pulled his pants on, but they remained unbuttoned, and he sat in the same place she'd left him.

Relief flooded her, even as fear trickled underneath. Would she be revealing too much when she handed him the binder? Would he see what she so desperately tried to keep hidden?

Inhaling a breath, she crossed the few feet separating them and perched on the mattress next to him.
"Here," she whispered, handing him the thick folder.

He glanced at her, his gaze steady and unwavering on her face. Searching. Though everything in her
demanded she protect herself from that too-knowing,
too-perceptive stare, she met it.

"What is it?" he asked, voice low, intense.

"Look," she instructed instead of answering.
"Please."

After another long second, he finally nodded and
accepted the binder. Her heart slammed against her
rib cage like a wild thing, reverberating in her head
and deafening her to everything but the incessant
pounding.

Slowly, he flipped the top open.

And froze.

Afraid to lift her gaze to his face—afraid of what
she'd glimpse there—she, too, studied the image of
one of his mixed-media collages. This one reflected
the tragedies of war. With haunting photographs,
pieces of metal that appeared to be machinery, newspaper and paint, he'd created a powerful work that,
even though it was a black-and-white copy, thrust
into her chest and seized every organ. She *felt* when
she looked at his art. Anger, grief, fear but also hope
and joy. Jesus, how could one man create such raw,
wild beauty? How could he walk away from it? Had it
been like cauterizing a part of himself? She couldn't
imagine...

Silent, Joshua flipped to the next page. A black-

and-white copy of a piece commentating on home-lessness. Another page. A work celebrating women, their struggle, their suffering, their strength, their beauty. Page after page of his art that both criticized and celebrated the human condition.

When he reached the last copy, he sat there, un-moving, peering down at it, unblinking.

"Why?" he rasped, the first word he'd spoken in the last ten minutes as he perused his past and what had once been his future.

She didn't pretend to misunderstand his question. "When I was researching you and your family for the first article, I came across several stories about you as an artist. From your college and local newspapers as well as several art columns. They carried pictures of your art. And they were so… *Good* is such an inad-equate choice. They were visceral. And to think you, Joshua Lowell, had created them…" She shrugged a shoulder. "I guess it became kind of an obsession. I hunted down any image of your work I could find. Finding out about this man who could drag this from his soul and share it with the world? I needed to talk to him, to discover how he'd become a CEO instead of an artist. And that's why I wanted the article to in-clude that side of you. Because I was struggling with reconciling the two."

"That man doesn't exist anymore," Joshua stated flatly. "You're searching for a ghost. He was buried fifteen years ago."

"I don't believe that," she countered. He glanced sharply at her, but she didn't tone down her vehemence. "You might have tried, but he trickles through when you help others follow their own dreams about art. When you support them and give your time and money toward them. If you'd truly put that man aside, he wouldn't help others who need him. That passion to educate people about this world may not have been exhibited in artwork these past years, but you still reveal it in your actions."

He shook his head, and despite the grim line of his full mouth, a tenderness entered his gaze. "You see what and who you want to, Sophie."

"No, I see you. This." She smoothed a hand over the image of his artwork. "This is you. A visionary. An activist and change agent in your own way. An *artist*." She tilted her head, studied his face. "What if your life doesn't end with Black Crescent? What if, after all these years, it's your time to live your own life, the one you left behind for family? A family that you owe nothing to but love and loyalty. You once said you couldn't abandon your family. But then you abandoned yourself. What's the worst that could happen if you followed your own delayed dreams, your own passions? Your mother will be okay and taken care of. And your brothers? If they choose to cut you out of their lives, then that's their problem and issues, not yours. Now's your time. And you never know. Maybe if given no other chance but to step up and assume the mantle of responsibility that you've worn for so long, your brothers might surprise you and do it."

She hesitated. Did she tell him all of it? In for a

penny and all that… Inhaling a deep breath, she held it, then exhaled. And leaped.

"I didn't tell you before now, but Christopher Harrison with the Tender Shoots nonprofit approached me about you at the gala. He read my article, saw the pictures of your art included in it. He wants to offer you your own show in Manhattan, at the Guggenheim. Not only to bring in money for the organization, but he would be excited about seeing you reemerge as the artist you were. Are."

For a moment—a quick, heart-stopping moment— a light glittered in his eyes. A light that could've been hope or joy. But then, in the very next, his hazel eyes dimmed. And disappointment squeezed her chest, her heart. He glanced away from her, staring at the far wall as if it revealed precious answers.

"That's not possible, and I'm not interested. You have no clue how it is to live under the weight of society's expectations," he murmured. His fingers curled into a fist atop the binder. But deliberately, he stretched them out, splaying them across the page— covering the image of his art. "You don't understand the burden of always knowing someone's waiting for you to misstep to prove that bad blood will out. It doesn't matter whether I continue to run Black Crescent or pick up a camera or paintbrush again. I can't escape, because I can't evade who I am. Joshua Lowell, Vernon Lowell's son."

She swallowed the silent sob of frustration, anger and grief. Grief for the man who believed he was forever tainted by the actions of his father. Who believed

the only road available to him was the one he trod—
even if it led to a future that wasn't his.

"Maybe not," she murmured, cupping his cheek
and turning his face toward her. "But maybe I can
help you bear the burden. Just a little."

Leaning forward, she brushed her lips across his,
then covered his mouth with hers. His groan vibrated
between them, before he turned, letting the binder
fall to the floor, and hauled her up the bed. He took
control of the kiss, crawling over her, finding his
place between her thighs.

And as he consumed them both with his burning
passion, she wept inside for him.

For the both of them.

Ten

"Josh, I'm heading home now," Haley announced from the doorway of his office. "Do you need anything before I leave?"

Joshua looked up from his computer. "No, I'm good."

Nodding, she stepped back, then paused, tilting her head to the side. "Everything okay with you?"

He leaned back in his chair, frowning. Other than a busy schedule and meetings all day, he was fine. He also had plans to meet Sophie at her apartment, so he was actually more than fine. But that, he kept to himself. "Yes, why do you ask?"

"You seem, I don't know—" her hazel eyes narrowed on him "—relaxed this past week. Something up I should know about?"

He snorted. "No, Haley. I'm good, like I said."

"Okay, if you say so."

"I say so."

"Well, not saying I don't believe you, but whatever—or whoever—has turned you into the Zen version of Joshua Lowell, give them—or her—my thanks." With an impish smile and arched eyebrow, she stepped back and shut the door behind her before he could reply.

"Brat," he muttered, but after a moment, chuckled. Yes, she was definitely the annoying younger sister he never asked for. But he didn't know what he'd do without her, either.

Glancing at the clock at the bottom of his monitor, he nodded. Six ten. Finishing a review of the report his CFO had sent him would take only about fifteen more minutes, twenty tops. Then he could head out.

When was the last time he'd looked forward to leaving his office that had become his second—hell, first—home? Not until Sophie. A lot of things in his life could be separated into two eras. Before the Scandal and, now, After Sophie.

God, when had she become that significant in his life?

The answer blazed bright and sure. From the moment she barged into his office, demanding and so beautiful.

From the release of the article, to her revelation about his supposed child, to her ice-thawing passion and kindness… She'd changed his world.

She'd changed him.

A kernel of fear rooted inside him, and try as he

might, he couldn't dislodge it. It'd been there since Monday night after she'd shocked him with the binder full of his previous artwork, and damn near taken him out with her body and the abandoned pleasure she'd offered him.

No one had ever taken the time to look further than the persona he presented. No one had bothered. Except for Sophie. She'd challenged him, as she'd been doing since their first meeting. Daring him to grab ahold of the dreams, the future he'd aborted when his father had disappeared. For a moment, he'd glimpsed what he could have, who he could be through her eyes. And the joy that had spread through him like the brightest and warmest of lights had been stunning. And terrifying.

Stunning because he hadn't felt such happiness in years—fifteen to be exact.

And terrified because he wanted it so badly. His old life back. The opportunity to work in his passion again. The possibility of his own show.

Sophie.

But he couldn't have any of them.

None of them were meant for him.

All he could do was be satisfied with the here and now, because it, too, would eventually end. Sophie would eventually leave him when she became discontented with what he could offer her. What he couldn't give her.

But he knew that going in. Everything ended. Everyone left.

Shaking his head, he frowned, refocusing on the

work he had left to finish. But then a notification for an email popped up on the bottom of his screen.

The frown deepened, as did an unnerving sense of dread.

He hesitated, his cursor hovering over the notice. Dammit, what was he doing? It could be anyone. His clients and some of his employees worked longer hours than him. The message could be from any one of them.

Clenching his jaw, he resolutely clicked on the notification.

Anonymous.

Just like the name on the message that had arrived in his inbox yesterday.

Congratulations, Papa! Your daughter can't wait to meet you!

He'd passed it off as some kind of joke. Since no one had contacted him about a possible child, and Sophie hadn't found anything more concrete yet, he'd assumed the DNA test had been a mistake. Or a way to just mess with him by inserting his name at the top. Wouldn't he know, somehow *feel*, if he had a child out there? Though it'd thrown him, he'd ignored the email yesterday…and hadn't told Sophie about it.

But now, he stared at another email from the same person. Disquiet settled over him like a suffocating weight. Trepidation churned in his gut, and his grip on his mouse tightened until the casing squeaked a threatening crack.

He didn't want to open it.

So he did.

Don't know why you're denying it. I paid good money to make sure you'd get the proof.

The words blurred, jumbled together, then leaped into startling clarity. They glared up at him, almost blinding him. Tearing his gaze from the message, he pushed from his chair and stalked across the room, thrusting his fingers through his hair. But he couldn't escape the image branded into his head.

I paid good money to make sure you'd get the proof.

There was only one person who'd brought an illegitimate child to his attention.

One person who'd provided him with the so-called proof.

Sophie.

Anger rolled through him like an ominous storm cloud spiked with bolts of lightning. Hot, heavy, sizzling.

He'd been so stupid. So goddamn blind.

What had been her endgame? Send him on this wild-goose chase, pretend to help him just to get close and what? Write a story on the whole journey? Paint him as some deadbeat? Or a pathetic father on the search for a child who wasn't his? That maybe didn't even exist?

Pain tried to course through him, but he blocked it. Allowed the fury to capsize it.

Fury was better. It razed everything to the ground. Including the fact that he'd started to trust this woman, and he'd been betrayed.

Again.

Sophie stepped off the elevator onto the second floor of the Black Crescent building. Anticipation danced a quick step inside her, and she smiled. Joshua would be surprised to see her there, since they'd planned to meet at her apartment later. But she couldn't wait. She'd finished the follow-up article and wanted to give him the first look at it before Althea saw it Friday morning.

God, this trod so close to her experience with Laurence. She'd made the mistake of granting him the opportunity to read her articles first. But unlike her ex, Joshua wouldn't use this as a chance to sabotage the story or have her change it to fit his needs or agenda. One, Joshua didn't have an agenda. But two, and most important, he wasn't Laurence.

Nerves trotted in her belly, but they didn't trump the happiness spilling through her veins. This week had revealed even more of the man she'd fallen so hard for.

Yes, she could admit it to herself.

She loved Joshua Lowell.

And no, he hadn't rescinded his "no relationships" condition, but he felt more for her than someone to warm his—or her—bed. She sensed it in his every small but genuine smile, the casual affection, the endearments, in the time he asked to spend with her.

God, did it make her pathetic that she was another woman believing she could change a man?

Probably.

But the knowledge didn't dim her smile as she knocked on his door, then pushed it open.

"Josh," she greeted, entering his inner sanctum. "I know we were supposed to meet at…" She trailed off, taking in the guarded, aloof expression she hadn't seen in a week. "What's wrong? Did something happen?"

She rushed forward to his desk, but drew to an abrupt halt when he rose, that glacial stare not melting or wavering from her face. No, it hardened, and dread curdled in her stomach. What the hell was going on here?

"Josh?" she whispered.

"Joshua," he corrected in an arctic voice that matched his gaze.

Only her hands flattened on his desk kept her from crumbling to the floor. But it couldn't prevent her heart from cracking down the middle and screams wailing from every jagged break.

"What's going on?" she rasped. "Why—"

Without shifting his contemptuous regard from her face, he slowly spun the monitor on his desk around to face her. She dragged her eyes from the stark lines and sharp angles that she'd just traced with her lips the night before and shifted them to the computer screen.

A thread of emails. From an address named Anonymous.

She skimmed them, her horror growing, the slick, grimy strands twisting around the happiness that had filled her only moments earlier, strangling it until only sickness remained. Bile surged up from her stomach, past her chest and raced for her throat. Convulsively, she swallowed it down.

Not because of what the emails stated; she had no idea who had sent them or what they were implying by paying to make sure Joshua had received the DNA test. Because she hadn't received any money. But obviously, just one glance at the anger and disdain in his green-and-gold eyes, and she knew—*she knew*—he believed she had.

The nausea swelled again with a vengeance.

"I don't know what this is supposed to mean," she said, reaching for a calm that had abandoned her the moment she'd stepped into this office. "No one gave me money to give you the DNA results. But you don't believe me," she added, voice curiously flat.

"What, Sophie? I'm supposed to believe you over my lying eyes?" he drawled, eyes snapping fire. "I wondered why you would show me the test when you were so adamant about protecting your research and sources." He loosed a harsh, serrated bark of ugly laughter. "Now I have my answer."

"You really think I would do this? Accept a bribe to trick you into believing you had a daughter?" she demanded, her own rage kindling, burning away the pain. For now. "For what? Why would I do that?"

"You're a reporter, Sophie. I don't know. An editorial piece that could grace the front of your paper might be a very good reason." A terrible half smile curved the corner of his mouth. "How would your editor in chief feel if she knew her star reporter resorted to underhanded tactics just to get a story?"

So much for the anger. Pain, red-hot and consuming, blazed a path through her. She could barely draw in a breath that didn't hurt. But she wouldn't allow him to see it. She'd given him everything—her trust, her faith...her love. And he'd shit over all of it.

No, he'd get nothing else. Most definitely not her tears or her pride. Fuck him.

"I don't know why I'm so surprised," she said, jerking her chin higher. "This is what you wanted. What you were waiting on. And that email is just the convenient excuse."

"Should I know what you're referring to?" he asked, the man who'd made her laugh, made her cry out in the most unimaginable pleasure, gone. And in his place stood the man of ice she'd originally met those weeks ago.

"You're so transparent, Joshua," she murmured, shaking her head. "You've just been waiting for me to screw up. To disappoint you. To leave you. Just like everyone else. But the sad part of it is I wouldn't have. I would've stayed by your side for as long as you asked. Longer. But you can't trust that. You can't possibly believe someone would put you first, would love you enough to never abandon or hurt you."

"Sophie," he growled, but she cut him off with a slash of her hand.

"No. You would rather self-sabotage and destroy what we had, what we could've had if you'd just let me love you and let yourself love. Instead, you would accuse me of something so horrible, so cruel that it's beneath me and definitely beneath you. You're nothing but a coward, Joshua Lowell." She shoved off the desk, silently promising her legs they could crumble later once she was in her car and away from this place, this man. But not now. "You've been running scared for so long that you can't even recognize when someone is running toward you and with you, not from you."

Pivoting, she focused on putting one foot in front of the other and not stumbling. Concentrated on just getting away. Even as part of her hoped, prayed he would call her name. Apologize. Take back the ugliness that had breathed in this office.

But he didn't. And another part of her broke.

As she reached the door, she paused.

Without looking back over her shoulder, she grabbed the doorjamb and stared straight ahead into the dim outer office.

"I love you, Joshua. When I didn't believe in it anymore, you showed me it could exist again for me. I don't regret that. But I do regret that you would rather hold on to the past than my heart. And for that, I pity you."

She pulled the door closed behind her.

Closing it on him...and who they could've been.

Eleven

"Well, if it isn't Joshua Lowell. Slumming it." Joshua glanced up from his whiskey to see a tall, lean but muscular man with dark brown hair and blue eyes sink down onto the stool next to his. "To what do we owe this honor?"

Ignoring the man and his irritating smirk, Joshua returned to his drink and stared blindly at the flat-screen television overhead, where a basketball game he couldn't care less about played. But anything was better than his empty, lonely apartment. Everywhere he looked, memories of Sophie bombarded him. In his living room. On his rug. In his kitchen. In his bed. It'd been only four hours since she'd left his office, her words ringing in the air long after she'd left.

I love you, Joshua... I do regret that you would

rather hold on to the past than my heart. And for that, I pity you.

She loved him. How could she? He'd warned her he didn't do relationships. Didn't do happily-ever-afters. She'd called him a coward, but he had his reasons. And they were good reasons. They were...

Damn. He rubbed the bridge of his nose, pinching it, before lifting the tumbler to his mouth for another sip.

Yeah, even boring games, the din of conversation and subpar alcohol was better than the memories as his only company. Still, he thought while he glanced at the guy next to him as he called the bartender by name and ordered a beer, that didn't mean he wanted to be chatted up by a stranger with a chip on his shoulder. That smart-ass greeting had clued Joshua in that this man with his hard eyes and harder smile wasn't a fan of his.

Fuck. He'd come to this bar in the neighboring town for some peace, not more judgment from a drunken asshole.

"I heard the rumor you were here drinking, but I didn't believe it. Daryl, get another round for Mr. Lowell," he called to the bartender. "He looks like he could use it."

"No, thank you," Joshua told Daryl. "I'm good with what I have here."

"What? My money isn't good enough for a Lowell?" he drawled, a steel edge to his question. No, not a question. A gauntlet thrown down on the bar top between them.

Too bad for him, Joshua didn't feel like picking it up. That required too much effort, and he was just too tired.

"Do I know you?" Joshua turned, facing the other man, who seemed vaguely familiar, but his mind couldn't place him. "Because if not, then can you just tell me what your problem is with me so I can go back to my drink?"

A faint snarl curled the corner of his mouth. "Why am I not surprised that you don't recognize me? Why would you? From that lofty tower you rule from, it would be difficult to distinguish between the peasants. Even the ones you had a hand in destroying." Before Joshua could reply, the guy stuck his hand out. "Zane Patterson. Maybe you know the last name, if not me."

Patterson. The whiskey turned to swill in his stomach, roiling. God, yes, he knew that name. It'd been the name of one of the families that had been his father's clients.

"Oh, so I see you do remember." Zane nodded. "I guess that makes you somewhat better than your father, who screwed us over and never looked back."

"Yes, I do, and yes, he did," Joshua agreed, earning an eyebrow arch from Zane. Had the other man expected him to deny the accusation? To defend Vernon. He silently snorted. Not in this lifetime. Or the next, if his father was indeed there instead of lying around some beach surrounded by younger women and mai tais.

"What are you doing here, Lowell?" Zane asked,

picking up the beer the bartender set in front of him. Sipping from the mug, he studied Joshua over the rim. "Drowning your woes, maybe?"

"Listen, I understand why you of all people can't stand the sight of me. But I'm here, just trying to have a drink. You can hate me from across the room."

"Still so high and mighty," Zane murmured. "Even after finding out you're no better than the rest of us. Worse, I'd say. You wouldn't catch me abandoning a kid of mine. But like father, like son, I guess."

Shock slammed into him, nearly toppling him from the stool. "What the hell did you just say to me?" he rasped.

A sardonic smile darkened Zane's face. "You heard me. Don't tell me the reporter didn't give you the DNA test results? I specifically chose Sophie Armstrong to share that with."

The shock continued to resonate through him like the drone of a thousand bees, but anger started to rush in like a tide, swallowing it. "You paid Sophie to make sure I received it?" he ground out.

"Paid her? Hell no. It was free of charge. And my pleasure." He again smiled, but it nowhere near reached his icy blue eyes. No, that wasn't correct. They weren't icy. Something volatile and...bleak darkened those eyes. Pain. If Joshua wasn't mired in it, he might not have been able to identify it. "Someone anonymously emailed the results to me," Zane continued, his level voice not reflecting the turmoil he would probably deny existed in his gaze. "And I just passed them along. The test spoke for itself, so

I really didn't give a damn who sent them. But whoever it was must've known I wouldn't mind paying it
forward. Your father and family destroyed my world,
my family." Gravel roughened his tone, and Zane
jerked his head away from Joshua. A muscle ticked
along his jaw as he visibly battled some emotion he
no doubt hated that Joshua glimpsed. After several
seconds, the other man returned his regard to Joshua,
his expression carefully composed. Too blank. "I was
only too happy to return the favor. Everyone believes
you're this perfect guy when you have a child out
there that you won't even take care of. I can't wait for
people to find out just who you really are."

Oh God.

He'd fucked up.

Numb, Joshua turned back to face the bar, Zane's
hurt scraping Joshua's skin, his bitter words buzzing
in his ears. He'd sent the DNA tests. Free of charge.
Sophie had been telling the truth. No one had paid
her to show him the results. She hadn't lied to him.

But… He'd known that, hadn't he?

Deep down, where that terrified, lonely and angry
twenty-two-year-old still existed, he'd known she
wouldn't have been capable of betraying him. She'd
been right about him; he was a coward. So scared she
would leave him like everyone else he'd loved, he'd
jumped on the first obstacle that had presented itself
to push her out the door. Save himself the pain of her
rejecting him and walking away from him.

Even though he'd known she could never do what
he'd accused her of. Not sweet, honorable, honest,

strong Sophie. She said that she knew him better than anyone else, but he also knew her. Fear had kept him from acknowledging it in his office, but the truth couldn't be denied. He did know her.

And he loved her.

He *loved* her.

She'd seen beyond his tainted past and who his father was and had accepted him, believed in him, when he hadn't even been able to do the same for himself. She'd seen him as blameless, as a hero for so many people, as an artist with a passion and a dream. Sophie had never given up on him.

Now it was time he didn't. Time he believed in himself.

In them.

Setting the drink on the bar, Josh reached into his jacket and removed his wallet. He threw down several bills that covered his drinks and a healthy tip before turning back to Zane.

"I'm sorry my father caused you and your family so much pain. He was greedy and selfish and had no thought whatsoever for who he would hurt. But I was every bit as much of a victim as you were. I lost my family, too. But I refuse to apologize or take on his guilt and shame anymore, though. I've tried to make amends for his sins. But I'm tired of it. I'm done."

Without pausing or waiting to hear what Zane Patterson had to say to that, he pivoted and strode out of the bar.

For the first time in a decade and a half, feeling...free.

* * *

"Dammit," Sophie muttered, jerking the strap of her laptop bag from the car door where it'd snagged. Huffing out a breath, she let it slip to the ground and reached in the back seat for the cardboard box that contained some of her personal items from her desk.

Tears stung her eyes as she scanned the framed photo of her and her mom on vacation at Myrtle Beach a couple of years ago, her favorite "only the strongest women become writers" coffee mug and several other knickknacks. She'd waited until almost everyone on her floor had left for the evening before she packed up most of the items and carried them to her car. Fewer questions that way. Especially since she hadn't yet informed her boss that she was leaving her job with the *Falling Brook Chronicle*.

It'd been her decision, and not one she made lightly.

And not because she feared Joshua would follow through with his subtle threat about informing Althea of being paid to pass on the DNA test. And also not because she was afraid her editor in chief would fire her after finding out she and Joshua had slept together.

No, she was leaving the paper and Falling Brook for herself.

Start over fresh.

Free of memories of Joshua and her own foolishness.

Maybe she'd return to Chicago. Or even go somewhere totally new, like Seattle. She'd visited once in college and had loved the eclectic and vibrant energy of the city…

"Sophie."

No. It couldn't be. Her stubborn, starved brain had conjured up his voice. She squeezed her eyes close, trying to banish it. The last thing she needed was to start imagining him when she was trying to let him go.

"Sophie, please. Can I have just a minute?"

Okay, this was no dream. Even her mind couldn't envision Joshua Lowell saying "please."

She carefully set her box back onto the seat, then pivoted.

And she really should've taken several more minutes to prepare herself for coming face-to-face with him after yesterday. God, it was so unfair. He'd stomped all over her heart. That should wear on a man. He should at least have new wrinkles. Bags under his eyes. Gray hair.

Horns.

But no, he was as beautiful as ever.

Damn him.

"What are you doing here, Joshua?"

"What is that?" he asked instead of answering, his gaze focused on the cardboard box before jumping to her face. "Are you planning on going somewhere, Sophie?"

"That isn't any of your business." Not anymore. Sighing, she shut the rear door and picked up her laptop bag. She'd just come back for the rest of her stuff later. "Now, please answer my question. What are you doing here?"

"I came to see you," he said.

She shrugged a shoulder, moving past him toward her apartment building. "Well, you've achieved that objective, so if you'll excuse me…"

A firm but gentle grip encircled her elbow, and she briefly closed her eyes, thankful her back was to him. He couldn't witness the pain and longing that streaked through her at his touch. She vacillated between ordering him to never put his hands on her again and throwing herself into his arms, begging him to hold her…to love her.

Why, yes. She was pathetic.

Deliberately, she stepped back, out of his hold. Then shifted back even farther so even his scent couldn't tease her.

Pride notched her chin up high as she forced herself to meet his gaze. A gaze that wasn't cold like the last time they'd been together. No, it was softer, even…tender.

She hardened her heart, made herself remember how he'd accused her of lying to him, betraying him. Made herself remember that he'd cracked her heart in so many fragments, she still hadn't been able to find all the pieces.

"Sophie, one minute. That's all I'm asking, and then if you want me to, I'll walk away and never bother you again."

"Thirty seconds," she shot back. That was what he'd given her the first time she'd bulldozed her way into his office.

As if he, too, recalled the significance, a small smile curved his mouth. "I'll take it." He rubbed a hand across the nape of his neck and moved forward, but at the last second, halted. Respecting the distance she'd placed between them. "Sophie, I'm sorry. I'm so sorry for not believing in you. For accusing you of selling me out. For jumping to conclusions and painting you as the villain. For looking at you through the lens of my past instead of seeing who you really are. You were right about me. I was so scared you would leave me so I used whatever excuse I could to push you away first. I would rather be alone than risk the chance of someone hurting me again, betraying me again. And I punished you for my fears, my shortcomings. I'll never forgive myself for letting you walk out that door believing that I thought you capable of that. I know words are inadequate, but, sweetheart, I'm so fucking sorry."

Her lungs hurt from her suspended breath. His apology reached beneath skin and bone to her bruised and wounded heart, cupped it. Soothed it.

But the words were a little too late. The damage had been done. And she couldn't undo the hurt, the humiliation. The rejection of her love.

Her rejection of herself.

"Joshua, a few years ago, I met a man. Fell in love with him," she whispered. "I didn't know it at the time, but he was using me for his own ends. Not that you've ever done that," she hurriedly added, because of all he'd done to her, Joshua was incapable of that kind of perfidy. It just wasn't in him. "But I almost lost my career—I almost lost myself—because I loved the wrong man. A man who didn't love me in return.

I did lose my way, though. And I promised myself I would never give up my job, my independence, my integrity, my soul for another man. The cost was too high, and I wasn't—I'm not—willing to pay it. But standing in your office last night, I found myself on the precipice of doing just that. I may not have betrayed you, but I almost betrayed myself. I won't put myself in that position again. I refuse to." She shook her head, a heavy grief of what could've been for them an albatross around her shoulders. "Thank you for coming here, but I don't need your apology. I know who I am. I know what I deserve. A man who loves and trusts me. Who won't ask me to be less so he can be secure. A life where I can have it all and not feel guilty because I compromised myself to get it."

"You do deserve all of that, Sophie," he rasped, the fierceness in his voice widening her eyes, leaving her shaken. "All of it and more. I—" He took that step toward her that he'd hesitated over moments ago. "I am that man who loves and trusts you. I'd never ask you to be less so I can be secure, because the greater you are, the happier you are, the more successful you are, the better I am as a man. The man who loves and supports you. Compromise? If you compromised who you are, I would never know the joy of having all of you, just as you are. Brilliant, strong, determined, driven, beautiful. Sweetheart—" he tunneled a hand through his hair, disheveling the short, dark blond strands "—you've shown me that I don't have to bear my father's burdens any longer. You've taught me that I'm not forgotten, that I am so much more than I ever believed possible. I thought what happened with my father fifteen years ago was the worst thing that could ever happen to me. But if it hadn't occurred, you wouldn't have written an article on it. You wouldn't have come crashing into my life. And, sweetheart, all the pain, all the fear, all the loss—I'd go through it all again in a heartbeat if it meant meeting you, touching you…loving you." He closed the distance between them and cradled her cheek. "If that box means you're leaving your job, please don't do it. That's a compromise you should never make."

Tears stung her eyes, and she choked on the hope that insisted on rising in her chest. She'd called him a coward yesterday, but now it was her who was terrified. Of being crushed again. Because unlike Laurence, he could destroy her, and though she would find a way to cobble herself together again, she wouldn't be whole.

No, she couldn't.

Not again.

As much as she loved him, she just…couldn't.

"Joshua, I'm sorry. I can't. I love you—I probably always will—but I'm not that strong. I…can't."

She couldn't contain her sob as she cupped his hand and turned her face into it. Kissed it.

Then fled into her apartment building.

Twelve

Joshua stood near the bank of elevators, the animated and excited hum of chatter from Black Crescent's lobby reaching him. Beyond the wall he stood behind congregated reporters and cameramen from the tristate area. All hungry and anticipating the announcement that Joshua had promised to deliver. Anything concerning Black Crescent Hedge Fund would've stirred their interest, but on a Saturday morning, coming from Joshua himself, who never did press conferences, they would've jumped on this tidbit. Just as he'd hoped.

The media expected a business-related statement. And they would receive that.

But so much more.

Joshua's future rode on this press conference.

"Ready, Josh?" Haley asked, laying a hand on his upper arm. Concern and just a bit of sadness darkened her hazel eyes. "Are you sure about this?"

He nodded. "I've never been more certain about anything in my life." He covered her hand with his and clasped it. "And just in case I've never said so before, thank you for everything you've been to this company and to me. Those first few years, I don't know if I would've been able to make it without you."

Tears glistened in her eyes, but, Haley being Haley, she tipped her chin up and cleared her throat. "You're right. You wouldn't have," she drawled.

He chuckled and, giving her hand one last squeeze, moved forward into the throng of media.

At his appearance, the noise reached a fever pitch as questions were lobbed at him from overeager journalists. But he ignored them as he stepped to the podium and microphone, scanning the crowded lobby for one person...

There.

Sophie stood in the middle, lovely and composed.

Relief barreled into him. He'd been afraid she wouldn't show up—had even placed a call to Althea to request Sophie's presence. But that hadn't guaranteed she would've agreed. Seeing her here, though, the anxiety that he'd fought off all morning kicked in the door of his calm. This was the most important moment of his life. Hell, he was fighting for his life—his future.

I love you—I probably always will—but I'm not that strong.

Her words, so final but so weary, echoed in his head. The resolve in her voice had set his heart pounding, terrified he'd lost her. But hope, his love for her and, yes, desperation refused to let him give up. He would go to war for her. He just had to hold on to her declaration of love. And his belief that she was stronger than both of them put together.

"Thank you for coming here today on such short notice," he said into the mic. Immediately, the voices hushed, but the excitement and tension crackled in the air. "I'm going to share my announcement and will take only a few questions at the end."

He inhaled, his eyes once more finding and locking onto Sophie. Her silver gaze met his, and he found the strength to continue there.

"Fifteen years ago, I took the helm of Black Crescent Hedge Fund after my father embezzled money from the company, nearly bankrupting it and devastating his clients and their families. Since that time, I've rebuilt the business and have tried to make reparations for his crimes. But today, I will be stepping down as CEO of Black Crescent."

A roar of disbelief filled the lobby and camera flashes nearly blinded him. Still, he kept his attention on Sophie, spying the shock and confusion that widened her eyes and parted her lips. Questions bombarded him, and he held up his hands, warding them off. Again, silence descended.

"Over the next few months there will be a search for my successor. He or she will be carefully hand-picked to replace me as CEO. I'm sure you're all wondering why I'm resigning. I plan to go back to my first love, my art. I gave it up to run Black Crescent, but I've decided to return to it. And possibly— if the woman I'm in love with will agree to marry me—to plan a wedding."

Again, the room erupted. But he cared only about Sophie's reaction, and his heart seized at the shock and tears and…and love. *Please, God, let that be love glistening in her gray eyes.*

"I let my pride and fear blind me and hold me hostage for far too long. And I'm praying that it doesn't cost me her love. I've spent too many years in my father's shadow, worrying what other people thought. If I was worthy enough. But she brought me out of the dark and into the light with her love. And because she loves me, I am worthy. And I want to spend the rest of my life proving that she didn't make a mistake by taking a chance on me. If she'll have me."

He stared at her, silently willing her to let him tell the world her identity. But more, silently asking her again for her forgiveness and her love. Her hand in marriage.

It seemed like an eternity passed as he stood behind that podium, reporters yelling at him, cameras flashing again and again. But still, he caught her nod. Caught that beautiful smile that lit up her face, her eyes and his heart.

"Sophie, will you come up here with me?"

She didn't hesitate, but wound a path through the throng, and like Moses with the Red Sea, they parted, letting her pass. He didn't pay attention to anyone but her. His heart swelling larger than his chest as she neared. And when his hand finally enfolded hers, something inside him that had been hollow, filled. That lost puzzle piece slotted into its place, and he was whole. Complete.

He drew her close, and closer still until she walked into his arms. Bending his head over hers, he pressed a kiss to her hair. A shiver worked through him and he didn't care who saw it. She was in his embrace again. Her scent enveloped him. She warmed him. And God, he'd been cold for so long.

Leaning back, he cupped her face, tipping her head back. The tears he'd glimpsed seconds ago tracked down her face, and he wiped them away with his thumbs, brushing his lips across her cheekbones, the bridge of her nose, her lips.

"Sophie Armstrong, I'm who I was meant to be with you. I was created to love you, and I not only cannot imagine a future without you, I don't want one without you in it. Would you do me the honor of being my wife?"

"Yes, Josh," she said without hesitation and with a certainty and confidence that erased the hurt, shame and pain that had dogged him for fifteen years. "I love you, and there's nothing I want more than to live by your side."

With reporters exploding into chaos around them, he claimed her mouth.

And his future.

* * * * *

Dynasties:
Seven Sins

It takes the betrayal of only one man
to destroy generations.
When a hedge fund hotshot vanishes with billions,
the high-powered families of Falling Brook
are changed forever.

Now seven heirs, shaped by his betrayal,
must reckon with the sins of the past.

Passion may be their only path to redemption.

Experience all Seven Sins!

Ruthless Pride *by Naima Simone*
Forbidden Lust *by Karen Booth*
Insatiable Hunger *by Yahrah St. John*
Hidden Ambition *by Jules Bennett*
Reckless Envy *by Joss Wood*
Untamed Passion *by Cat Schield*
Slow Burn *by Janice Maynard*

Available May through November 2020!

WE HOPE YOU ENJOYED
THIS BOOK FROM

HARLEQUIN
DESIRE

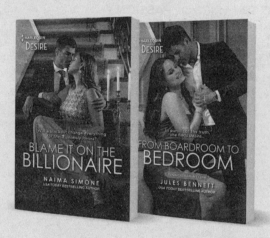

*Luxury, scandal, desire—welcome to
the lives of the American elite.*

Be transported to the worlds of oil barons, family dynasties,
moguls and celebrities. Get ready for juicy plot twists,
delicious sensuality and intriguing scandal.

6 NEW BOOKS AVAILABLE EVERY MONTH!

COMING NEXT MONTH FROM

DESIRE

Available June 2, 2020

#2737 THE PRICE OF PASSION
Texas Cattleman's Club: Rags to Riches • by Maureen Child
Rancher Camden Guthrie is back in Royal, Texas, looking to rebuild his life as a member of the Texas Cattleman's Club. The one person who can help him? Beth Wingate, his ex. Their reunion is red-hot, but startling revelations threaten their future.

#2738 FORBIDDEN LUST
Dynasties: Seven Sins • by Karen Booth
Allison Randall has long desired playboy Zane Patterson. The problem? He's her brother's best friend, and Zane won't betray that bond, no matter how much he wants her. Stranded in paradise, sparks fly, but Allison has a secret that could tear them apart...

#2739 UPSTAIRS DOWNSTAIRS TEMPTATION
The Men of Stone River • by Janice Maynard
Working in an isolated mansion, wealthy widower Farrell Stone needs a live-in housekeeper. Ivy Danby is desperate for a job to support her baby. Their simmering attraction for one another is evident, but are their differences too steep a hurdle to create a future together?

#2740 HOT NASHVILLE NIGHTS
Daughters of Country • by Sheri WhiteFeather
Brooding songwriter Spencer Riggs is ready to reinvent himself. His ex, Alice McKenzie, is the perfect stylist for the job. Years after their wild and passionate romance, Alice finally has her life on track, but will their sizzling attraction burn them both again?

#2741 SCANDALOUS ENGAGEMENT
Lockwood Lightning • by Jules Bennett
To protect her from a relentless ex, restauranteur Reese Conrad proposes to his best friend, Josie Coleman. But their fake engagement reveals real feelings, and Josie sees Reese in a whole new way. And just as things heat up, a shocking revelation changes everything!

#2742 BACK IN HIS EX'S BED
Murphy International • by Joss Wood
Art historian Finn Murphy has a wild, impulsive side. It's what his ex-wife, Beah Jenkinson, found so attractive—and what burned down their white-hot marriage. Now, reunited to plan a friend's wedding, the chemistry is still there... and so are the problems that broke them apart.

HDCNM0520

*To protect her from a relentless ex, restaurateur Reese
Conrad proposes to his best friend, Josie Coleman.
But their fake engagement reveals real feelings, and
Josie sees Reese in a whole new way. And just as things
heat up, a shocking revelation changes everything!*

Read on for a sneak peek at
Scandalous Engagement
by USA TODAY *bestselling author Jules Bennett.*

"What's that smile for?" he asked.

She circled the island and placed a hand over his heart. "You're
just remarkable. I mean, I've always known, but lately you're just
proving yourself more and more."

He released the wine bottle and covered her hand with his…and
that's when she remembered the kiss. She shouldn't have touched
him—she should've kept her distance because there was that look
in his eyes again. Where had this come from? When did he start
looking at her like he wanted to rip her clothes off and have his
naughty way with her?

"We need to talk about it," he murmured.

It. As if saying the word *kiss* would somehow make this situation
weirder. And as if she hadn't thought of anything else since *it* had
happened.

"Nothing to talk about," she told him, trying to ignore the warmth
and strength between his hand and his chest.

"You can't say you weren't affected."

"I didn't say that."

He tipped his head, somehow making that penetrating stare even
more potent. "It felt like more than a friend kiss."

Way to state the obvious.

"And more than just a practice," he added.

Josie's heart kicked up. They were too close, talking about things that were too intimate. No matter what she felt, what she thought she wanted, this wasn't right. She couldn't ache for her best friend in such a physical way. If that kiss changed things, she couldn't imagine how anything more would affect this relationship.

"We can't go there again," she told him. "I mean, you're a good kisser—"

"Good? That kiss was a hell of a lot better than just good."

She smiled. "Fine. It was pretty incredible. Still, we can't get caught up in this whole fake-engagement thing and lose sight of who we really are."

His free hand came up and brushed her hair away from her face. "I haven't lost sight of anything. And I'm well aware of who we are…and what I want."

Why did that sound so menacing in the most delicious of ways? Why was her body tingling so much from such simple touches when she'd firmly told herself to not get carried away?

Wait. Was he leaning in closer?

"Reese, what are you doing?" she whispered.

"Testing a theory."

His mouth grazed hers like a feather. Her knees literally weakened as she leaned against him for support. Reese continued to hold her hand against his chest, but he wrapped the other arm around her waist, urging her closer.

There was no denying the sizzle or spark or whatever the hell was vibrating between them. She'd always thought those cheesy expressions were so silly, but there was no perfect way to describe such an experience.

And kissing her best friend was quite an experience…

Don't miss what happens next in…
Scandalous Engagement
by USA TODAY *bestselling author Jules Bennett.*

Available June 2020 wherever
Harlequin Desire books and ebooks are sold.

Harlequin.com

HDEXP0520